"What kind of per... She repeated his... "Hardworking, disciplined, focused. Very successful—one of the top five bankers in the world, probably..."

"You make me sound like a machine," he said, and a note of something like bitterness crept into his voice.

Kiloran's voice softened. "You're no machine, Adam—I can assure you of that." She drew a deep breath, because this kind of thing wasn't easy to say, out cold, to a man who technically was your lover but who didn't remember a thing about you. "You're a warm, giving lover." She swallowed. "The best lover I've ever had..."

*Getting down to business
in the boardroom...and the bedroom!*

A secret romance, a forbidden affair,
a thrilling attraction...

What happens when two people work together
and simply can't help falling in love—
no matter how hard they try to resist?

Find out in our series of stories
set against working backgrounds.

This month in
Back in the Boss's Bed by Sharon Kendrick

Hotshot businessman Adam Black is
Kiloran's new boss—and the most devastatingly
attractive man she has ever met. It isn't long
before he's made love to her, but he won't let
her close. Then an accident leaves Adam with
memory loss, and he must depend on Kiloran
to nurse him back to health....

Sharon Kendrick

BACK IN THE BOSS'S BED

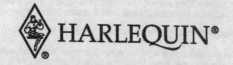

TORONTO • NEW YORK • LONDON
AMSTERDAM • PARIS • SYDNEY • HAMBURG
STOCKHOLM • ATHENS • TOKYO • MILAN • MADRID
PRAGUE • WARSAW • BUDAPEST • AUCKLAND

If you purchased this book without a cover you should be aware
that this book is stolen property. It was reported as "unsold and
destroyed" to the publisher, and neither the author nor the
publisher has received any payment for this "stripped book."

With thanks to Edward Heckels
for all his invaluable advice—
this book is for him and for all future Heckels.

Vote for Edward!

ISBN 0-373-12322-1

BACK IN THE BOSS'S BED

First North American Publication 2003.

Copyright © 2003 by Sharon Kendrick.

All rights reserved. Except for use in any review, the reproduction or
utilization of this work in whole or in part in any form by any electronic,
mechanical or other means, now known or hereafter invented, including
xerography, photocopying and recording, or in any information storage
or retrieval system, is forbidden without the written permission of the
publisher, Harlequin Enterprises Limited, 225 Duncan Mill Road,
Don Mills, Ontario, Canada M3B 3K9.

All characters in this book have no existence outside the imagination of
the author and have no relation whatsoever to anyone bearing the same
name or names. They are not even distantly inspired by any individual
known or unknown to the author, and all incidents are pure invention.

This edition published by arrangement with Harlequin Books S.A.

® and TM are trademarks of the publisher. Trademarks indicated with
® are registered in the United States Patent and Trademark Office, the
Canadian Trade Marks Office and in other countries.

Visit us at www.eHarlequin.com

Printed in U.S.A.

CHAPTER ONE

ADAM BLACK'S grey eyes glittered like sunlight on a wintry sea. 'So, Vaughn?' he questioned softly.

From his wheelchair, the old man looked up at the tall, dark man who dominated the room. 'I hate asking anyone for favours!' he rasped. 'Even you.'

'And I hate granting them,' said Adam, his hard mouth relaxing by just a fraction as he acknowledged the old man's indomitable character, recognising in him something of himself. 'But in your case, I'll make an exception. What's up?'

There was a pause. 'You remember my granddaughter?' Vaughn demanded. 'Kiloran? She's been running the business—only she's come up against problems. Big problems.'

Kiloran? Adam let his memory stray back, then back further still, and a fleeting image of a green-eyed girl in pigtails flitted in and out of his mind. A little princess of a girl, despite the pigtails and the grubby jeans. But the Laceys had been rich, as rich as Adam had been poor—and the power of money had clung to her like a second skin.

'Yeah, I remember her. Vaguely.' He frowned. 'Though she would have just been a kid at the time. Nine—ten maybe.'

'That was a long time ago. She's not a kid anymore.

She's twenty-six, and a woman now. Kiloran is my daughter's child,' added Vaughn, his eyes half closed with reminiscence. 'You must remember her mother. Everyone remembers Eleanor.'

Adam stilled.

Oh, yes. This particular memory snapped into crystal-sharp focus. He had locked it away, as he'd locked so many things away over the years, but Vaughn's words were the key to the door, and now it swung open. 'Yes, I remember Eleanor,' he said slowly.

It had been every teenage boy's fantasy, except maybe his.

He had been eighteen, all long legs and muscle— strong as an ox and tanned as a berry. The summer had been hot—too hot to load boxes all day, but that had been his job, his way out of the dark tunnel his life had become. God, it seemed so long ago.

Eleanor must have been about…what? Forty? Maybe younger, maybe older—it was hard to tell with women of a certain age. All Adam had known was that she'd been a looker.

The men working in the warehouse had just stopped what they'd been doing, their breath hot with lust when Eleanor had walked by, as walk by she so often had—making excuses to visit the factory, wearing tiny denim shorts and a T-shirt which had been rucked tight across her breasts. The beautiful widow—she might have been called the Black Widow, if her hair hadn't been the colour of spun gold.

Adam had listened to them talk. A tease, they'd

called her. Look but don't touch. She was protected by the power of her position. The boss's daughter.

She'd known the power of her own sexuality, too— it had radiated off her like a shimmering heat and it had fuelled many fantasies those hot summer nights.

But not Adam's.

Something about her had made him recoil. Something about her hooded, predatory look had made him look away. Maybe it had reminded him too much of what he had left behind at home.

She'd noticed him, of course. He'd been different. He'd been bright and smart. Stronger and bigger and fitter and more ruggedly handsome than any of the permanent loaders. And she'd noticed the way he hadn't noticed her. Some women liked a challenge.

She'd waited until his last week there—presumably not to give herself time to get bored, or to risk angering her father. Vaughn had been a stickler for sticking to the rules and a penniless kid from a rough family on the wrong side of town had not been for his daughter, not in any way.

But Eleanor had had other ideas.

She'd brought him a beer one baking afternoon, when the ground had scorched your feet—the first taste of liquor he had ever had. On such a hot day, it had been too tempting to refuse and it had filled him with a kind of warm wildness. But he had stayed his distance, his eyes as wary as a cornered animal when she had patted the haystack where she'd lain sprawled.

'Come over here,' she purred.

'I'm fine where I am,' he said.

She didn't like being refused, nor did she take the hint. She knew what she wanted and she wanted him.

She was wearing a flowery little shirt that day—a teensy little thing with buttons all the way down the front, and when she began to brazenly pop them open, one by one, her green eyes meeting his, he froze.

Maybe there wasn't another man on the planet who would have refused what Adam was so freely being offered, but Adam wasn't most men. He had seen what weakness and excess could do. Wasn't his presence here doing a dead-end job the very result of it?

Nothing was said. He simply picked up his denim shirt and thanked her for the beer, and strolled out into the mercilessly hot sunshine. He didn't see her look of frustrated lust, but he felt it. It was the first time it had happened to him, but it wouldn't be the last.

He gave Vaughn a cool look. 'Yes, I remember your daughter. What happened to her?'

Vaughn gave a wheezy laugh. 'She did what she wanted to do—married a millionaire and moved to Australia.' He shrugged. 'Said she wanted a better life—and you know what women are like.'

There was a pause, while Adam remembered the woman he had taken for dinner on his last night in New York. A sloe-eyed beauty who had cooed into his ear that what he didn't know about women could be written on the back of a postage stamp and still leave room to spare! He hadn't made love to her—his body had been willing but his mind had not, for he had never been able to separate the intellectual from the physical. She had cried. Women always cried when they couldn't get what they wanted, and mostly they wanted him. It was not an arrogant assessment of his attributes as a man and as a lover, it was fact—plain and simple.

'Yes, I know what women are like,' he said shortly. 'So Kiloran stayed, did she?'

Vaughn nodded. 'She went away and then came back. She missed the house.' He gave a look of pride. 'She loves it just the same as I do. But loving a house is not the same as running a business. I was a fool to let myself think she was capable of taking charge. Yes, she had experience of company life—but it was too big a project to handle.' He shook his head. 'She twisted me round her little finger—the way she can twist any man around her little finger! And Kiloran always knows best!'

Adam didn't point out the glaringly obvious. That in this instance she had failed completely in her judgement.

'You said you weren't working at the moment,' growled Vaughn. 'So, in theory, you have a little time on your hands.'

Adam stared unseeingly out at the sunlit gardens beyond which seemed to stretch on and on as far as the eye could see. The Lacey mansion had always seemed like a different world when he had been young—like an unattainable mountain to climb—only now he was a part of that world. He hadn't been back here since the day he'd left—not to this house, nor the pitiful version of a house he had grown up in. And now his two worlds had merged in the way that fate so often decreed they did. It felt strange, he thought. Had it been a mistake to come?

'That's right,' he agreed. 'I don't start my new job until next month.'

Vaughn drew himself up, his stiff body moving awkwardly. 'I want you to make Lacey's what it was, Adam. If anyone can do it—you can. Before I die, I want my good name to stand and I want this firm to carry on. For Kiloran's sake. Will you do that?'

Adam's dark eyebrows knitted together. 'But how's Kiloran going to feel about it? If she's heading up your company, how's she going to adapt to taking her orders from me? Unless.' His eyes took on a watchful wariness. 'Unless you want her out of the way, of course. You're not planning to sack her, are you?'

Vaughn let out a wheezing laugh. 'Sack her? I'd sooner take on the devil himself than risk that!'

'But, you know—' Adam's grey eyes grew thoughtful and flinty '—if it's as bad as you seem to think it is, and you want results, then I'm going to have to be tough with her.'

The old man smiled. 'Be as tough as you like. Maybe I've been too soft with her in the past. Show her who's in the driving seat, Adam. She needs to know—she's a stubborn little thing.'

Adam digested this in silence, knowing that no one could match *him* for stubbornness. And he wondered whether perhaps it *was* Vaughn's intention to use him to oust his stubborn granddaughter from her position of power. Maybe that was one of his reasons for approaching him. Get someone else to do your dirty work for you.

But he put it out of his mind. Personalities didn't come into it and neither did other people's agendas.

There were facts and you acted on those facts. Didn't matter who said what, or to whom. Didn't matter if Kiloran Lacey was a clone of her mother and started fluttering her pretty eyelashes at him, trying to get her own way. She would soon find out, just as her mother had done, that he was *not* the kind of man she could twist around her little finger. From now on he was going to decide what was best, and if she didn't like it—well, that was just too bad.

Vaughn gave a satisfied nod and pressed the bell on the side of his wheelchair once more, and the door was opened to reveal a middle-aged woman, bearing a tray containing two glasses and a bottle of champagne, cooling in an ice bucket.

'Ah, Miriam,' said Vaughn. 'Pour Mr Black a drink, would you?'

Adam hid a smile. So the old man had been confident he'd agree, had he? And why not? Didn't he owe Vaughn Lacey for a favour given to a young boy in trouble, such a long time ago? He watched as Miriam deftly dealt with the drinks. She wore a black dress with a white collar—clearly some kind of uniform. He hadn't seen such an old-fashioned set-up for years, but, admittedly, he had been living in America, which was altogether a more meritocratic society.

His eyes were drawn to an exquisite Augustus John etching, which hung on the wall, and he pursed his lips together thoughtfully. That piece of artwork alone must be worth a cool couple of million. He wondered how much else around the place was existing on past glories and how well Vaughn and his granddaughter would be able to adapt if any cut-backs were going to be necessary.

But now was not the time to start asking questions like that. He took the drinks from Miriam, and when she had let herself out he handed one to the old man and then raised his own, touching it to the other, the chink of crystal sounding as pure as the ringing of a bell.

'To success. To the resurrection of Lacey's,' he murmured, raising the drink to his lips and wondering just what the hell he had let himself in for.

Vaughn gave a tight smile. 'I'll send for Kiloran.'

CHAPTER TWO

KILORAN smoothed her clammy palms down over her hips, feeling suddenly and inexplicably nervous. The corridor leading to the boardroom seemed to go on forever, a corridor which she had walked down countless times—so why the nerves?

Her grandfather had telephoned her at the house and asked her to meet him. Immediately. It had sounded more like a command than a request and he had spoken in a terse, almost abrupt way, which didn't sound like him at all.

Was he about to tell her that he didn't think there was any point carrying on? That they should call in the creditors? The end of the company and all that went with it?

A cold sweat broke out on her forehead as she pushed open the door of the boardroom, thrown off her guard as soon as she registered that her grandfather was not alone.

For a man stood, surveying her with a lazy, yet judgemental air. The kind of man who would make any woman's heart miss a beat and whose expression would fill her with foreboding.

She turned to the familiar figure in the wheelchair. 'Grandfather?' she said uncertainly.

'Ah, Kiloran,' murmured her grandfather. 'This is Adam. Adam Black. Do you remember him?'

It was like a little pebble being dropped into a pond. Slowly, the ripples of memory spread across Kiloran's mind. She frowned.

Adam Black.

Of course she remembered him.

True, she had only been young, but some men came along who were so unforgettable that their image was scored deep in the psyche, and had been at an impressionable age. Reading stories about knights in shining armour who carried off with them the damsel in distress to some unnamed and yet pleasurable fantasy.

Adam Black had seemed to fit the role perfectly, and—judging from the female workers at Lacey's— Kiloran had not been the only one to think so. Hadn't groups of them found excuses to go to the loading bay, in order to catch a glimpse of the bare-chested man, as he'd effortlessly lifted great boxes of soap into the lorries? Hadn't even her mother remarked that he was a fine-looking boy?

And so it was with astonishing and rather disturbing ease that Kiloran was able to recall Adam Black perfectly.

She turned her head to look at him.

The years had not just been kind to him, they had treated him with the deference usually only given to the chosen few.

The body was lean and lithe, his skin kissed with the faintest tan. The hair was still jet-black—thick and abundant as it had ever been with only a faint tracing of silver around his temples. The grey eyes were narrowed and watchful. He looked—not exactly unfriendly, but not exactly brimming over with *bonhomie*, either, and he was dressed in an immaculate charcoal-grey suit, as if he was ready for business.

She remembered the young man wearing nothing but a pair of faded denims, his bronzed back dripping with the sweat of his labours, and it seemed hard to connect him with *this* man, who stood before her now, a dark study of arrogant respectability.

Kiloran's heart had begun to thunder beneath the thin silk of her dress, but the voice of reason began to clamour in her head.

Why on earth was he here?

And her childhood crush was eclipsed by the sudden crowding in of facts. She suddenly realised just why his name had sounded so familiar—and not just because he had spent one summer doing hard, manual work for her grandfather. She made the connection, and she was even more confused.

Adam Black—*the* Adam Black—was here in *her* boardroom? The man that the investment journals called 'The Shark' because of his cold and cutting ways? She had read about him, in the way that anyone in the business would have done. She had seen him quoted in the papers and read about him in the magazines which covered big mergers and acquisitions. And seen his regular appearances in the gossip columns, too. The camera loved him and so did women, beautiful women, invariably. He had acquired a reputation for loving and leaving—though maybe not for loving, but certainly for *leaving*.

So why was he *here*? She stared at him in confusion.

'You remember my granddaughter?' Vaughn was saying. 'Kiloran Lacey?'

Adam gave a brief, curt nod. 'It was a long time ago,' he murmured.

A very long time ago. Certainly, his snatched, snapshot memory of a girl in pigtails bore no resemblance to the woman sitting at the huge, round table wearing a dress as darkly green as her eyes. Her long, shapely legs were outlined by the thin fabric, but not even her magnificent legs could detract from the lush breasts, the silky material of the dress doing very little to disguise their almost shocking fullness.

He had remembered fair hair, tightly bound in pigtails, but the colour of her hair was as pure as spun gold, although most of it was caught back in a knot. She had her mother's hair, he thought fleetingly. And her mother's eyes—or at least they were the same colour. Because the eyes which returned his stare were cool and intelligent and assessing, not hot and hungry and predatory like her mother's. But women wore different masks, didn't they? Who knew what kind of woman Kiloran Lacey really was?

But outwardly, at least, she was perfect.

Her skin was as pale as clotted cream, which contrasted so vividly with her rich green eyes. She had the kind of natural beauty which, in another age, would have had artists clamouring to paint her.

Her lips were wide and lush and full, and held the merest suggestion of a pout of displeasure as she looked at him as if he had absolutely no right to be there. And that little pout stirred at his senses in a way it had no right to. Or maybe it was the unsmiling look on her face. Adam was used to an instant response from women, and for once he wasn't getting it.

'Nice to see you,' he said shortly.

Kiloran kept her voice steady. 'Would someone mind telling me what's going on?' She gave him a polite smile. 'I don't understand why you're here, Mr Black.'

'Call me Adam.' His mouth thinned into a bland smile. 'Please.'

Something about his superior, almost *arrogant* self-assurance made Kiloran begin to simmer. How dared he look as though he had every right to stand around lording it and as if she—*she*—were in some way superfluous! She felt like calling him something far more uncomplimentary than his first name, but she drew a deep breath. 'Adam,' she managed steadily. 'This is something of a surprise.'

'I've asked Adam to establish the full extent of the embezzlement,' said her grandfather.

Embezzlement. There it was. Such a horrible word, and no less horrible because it was true. A fact. A smooth-talking accountant with a convincing line in lies and she had fallen for it, hook, line and sinker.

'But I've been working on that myself,' she objected. 'You know I have.'

'And you're involved, Kiloran,' drawled Adam. 'So I'm afraid it isn't quite that easy.'

Her heart missed a beat as she stared at him incredulously. 'Are you trying to suggest that I've stolen from my own company?'

He shook his dark head. 'Of course not. You weren't involved in the process itself,' he said blandly. 'But, unlike me, you won't be able to take an impartial overview of the situation.'

'I think you underestimate me,' she shot back and she met the answering look in his eye which said as clearly as if he had spoken it, I think not.

'Why don't I leave the two of you in peace?' said her grandfather hurriedly, and began to manoeuvre the wheels of his chair in the direction of the door.

Kiloran scarcely noticed him leave, her breath was coming in short and indignant little blasts, which was making her chest rise and fall as if she had been running in a particularly fast race.

Adam wished to hell that he had the authority to tell her to put a jacket on, but what reason could he give? That he found the sight of her moving breasts too distracting? That her hair was too shiny clean and blonde and her lips positively X-rated? That the silken look of her white and golden skin made it seem a sheer crime to have it covered in anything other than a man's lips?

Instead he curved his mouth into the sardonic smile which would have made people who knew him well have serious misgivings about his next words.

'Your grandfather asked me to review your financial

position,' he said bluntly. 'And I've had a preliminary look at the figures.'

There was a simmering silence while she looked at him. 'And?'

The grey eyes became as steely as his voice. 'I suspect that it's worse than even he thought.' He paused just long enough for her to realise just how serious it was. And then he remembered Vaughn's kindness, remembered too that this woman was his granddaughter. He forced a smile.

'I'm afraid that we're going to have to make a few changes round here.' The silence became slightly tighter still before he delivered his final blow. 'Because, without a miracle, I'm afraid your company will go bust, Kiloran.'

CHAPTER THREE

Without a miracle, your company will go bust.

ADAM BLACK fixed her with a cool, challenging look and Kiloran stared at him, trying not to be lulled by the stormy beauty of his eyes.

'Aren't you exaggerating just a little?'

He observed the cool, almost haughty look she was giving him and for a moment he almost relished wiping that proud look from her face before plucking a sheaf of papers from his briefcase and flicking a dismissive hand in their direction.

'Have a chair,' he drawled, in the kind of tone which suggested that she didn't have a choice.

'Thanks,' she said stonily, thinking that he seemed to have acquired the ability to make her feel like a stranger in her own boardroom.

He sat down in the chair beside hers and his mouth curved. 'So you think I'm exaggerating, do you? Tell me, have you read these papers?'

'Of course I've read them!'

'Then surely you can be in no doubt about just how bad things are?'

'Do you think I'm stupid?'

He gave a cynical smile. 'Take my advice, honey. Never ask an open question like that. You're giving me the opportunity to say yes.'

'Then say it! I'm not afraid of your answer,' she said proudly.

He sighed with barely concealed impatience even though she looked very beautiful when she tilted her chin like that and the eyes sparked a witchy green fire. This was what happened when you worked with family firms—people behaved as if they owned the place, which, of course, they did. If Kiloran Lacey had been any other employee—no matter what her position in the company—he would have told her to stop wasting his time, to shut up and just listen.

'If anything, you've been guilty of mismanagement,' he said. 'Stupidity would imply that you had ignored advice, and I'm assuming you didn't?' He raised a dark, arrogant eyebrow. 'Or did you? Did anyone warn you that your company accountant had been salting away funds for his own private Swiss bank account, Kiloran?'

'Of course they didn't!'

'And you didn't notice?'

Now he was making her *feel* stupid. Very stupid. 'Obviously not.'

'Indeed.' Reflectively, he brushed the tip of his finger against his lips and subjected her to an unhurried appraisal. 'So what happened? Did you take your eye off the ball? Or weren't you watching the ball in the first place?'

He made her sound like a fool, and she was no fool. Kiloran knew that she had been guilty of a lack of judgement, but she was damned if she was going to have this supercilious man jumping to conclusions when he didn't know a damned thing about her! And looking at her in that cool, studied way, the thick, dark lashes shielding the grey eyes, making her feel she'd been caught momentarily off balance.

'You're full of questions, Mr Black—'

Questions which she seemed very good at evading, he acknowledged thoughtfully. So did that mean she had something to hide? 'I thought you were going to call me Adam.'

'If you insist.'

'Oh, I do,' he responded. 'I do.'

His dark face momentarily relaxed into one of lazy mockery. Kiloran swallowed, feeling out of her depth and it was a curious sensation. Men didn't usually faze her—even exceptionally good-looking men like this one, though she had never met a man quite like Adam Black. The aura of power and success radiated off him, but she was damned if she was going to be cowed by that. 'Perhaps it's time you provided me with a few answers yourself,' she said quietly.

He raised his eyebrows, trying to ignore the way her lips folded into pink petals. So she was trying to pull rank, was she? Hadn't it sunk in just how precarious her situation was? How people's livelihoods were at risk? Or was she just thinking of her own, spoilt little self?

He decided to humour her. Maybe if he gave her enough rope she would hang herself. 'And what exactly do you want to know, *Kiloran*?'

His voice was a steely honey-trap, but Kiloran let it wash over her. 'Just why my grandfather has called you in?'

Dark brows were knitted together. 'I should have thought that was obvious—he wants me to help you get out of the mess—'

'I've created?'

'Helped to create,' he amended.

'Please don't patronise me—'

'Patronise you?' Adam had had enough. 'Listen, if I were patronising you, you'd soon know about it!' He leaned forward by a fraction, then wished he hadn't because she smelt of some evocative scent—something flowery and delicate which shivered over his senses—and he jerked back as if someone had stung him. 'You know damned well why he's called me in!'

'Oh, yes—your reputation for getting things done is legendary.' She paused. 'But that doesn't explain why you've condescended to take on such a lowly assignment.'

His eyes glittered—what had he thought about giving her enough rope? 'Well, well, well—that sounds like a pretty fundamental problem to me,' he mused. 'If you consider your own company to be "lowly".'

'That's not what I meant, and you know it!' He was twisting everything she said! 'Just that you usually deal with far bigger ventures than this one!'

'Maybe I wanted a change.' He looked towards the large French windows, which overlooked the garden, where the view was as pretty as something from a picture, distracting enough, but far less distracting than the whispering movement of her silk as she crossed one bare brown leg over the other. 'A change of scene. A little country air.'

Kiloran felt the breath catch in her throat and it felt as if someone were tiptoeing over her grave. He was uncannily echoing her own sentiments and suddenly this seemed like trespass in more than one way—now

he was coveting her land as well as her company!
'How much are you being paid?'

Adam recognised the implied insult. So that was
how she still saw him, was it—the poor boy from the
wrong side of town who was not worthy to sit at the
same table as the princess? But his face remained as
coolly impassive as before. 'That's none of your business!' he said silkily.

'Oh, I think it is.'

His smile became bland, and the tone in his voice
quietly emphatic. He was damned if he was going to
tell her that he wasn't being paid a penny! Let her
think what she liked of him. 'Sorry.' He shook his
head. 'It's a private deal between your grandfather and
me. And while I am in charge, it will remain that way.'

While I am in charge. Kiloran stared at him as if
he'd suddenly started speaking in a foreign language!

'You mean—I'm going to be answerable to you?'

'I'm afraid you are.' He shrugged as he saw her
green eyes widen with genuine shock and for a moment he felt an unwilling tug of empathy. 'That's what
generally happens in situations like this.'

All the control which had seemed to be slipping
away from her ever since she had discovered Eddie
Peterhouse's defection now slid away from her entirely, and most of all she felt a sinking sense of hurt.
Why hadn't her grandfather spoken to her first?
Checked whether she would object to having this im-
passive-faced man waltzing in and taking charge of
everything. Including, it seemed—*her*!

She fixed her expression to one of studied calm. Let
him see that a one-off error of judgement did not mean

that she couldn't be as professional as he was. 'So where do we begin?' she asked coolly.

There was a pause. 'Why don't we start with you telling me something about yourself,' he said unexpectedly.

Something in the way he said it threatened her equilibrium. It sounded like the kind of question a man asked on a date, when he wanted to get to know you better, and this was certainly no date. 'Like what?'

He wanted to know what her golden hair would look like when it was freed to tumble down over the luscious swell of her breasts. He wanted to know if she cried out when she came. He wanted... 'Why, your job history, of course,' he replied evenly.

Some distracting darkening in his eyes made it difficult for her to concentrate. She swallowed. 'I went into the City, straight from university, stayed in my first job for three years and was working for Edwards, Inc. when Grandfather got ill—and the rest you know. The usual route.'

He said nothing for a moment. Usual for most people, maybe—and especially for privileged little princesses like Kiloran Lacey. Nothing like his own hard, clawing journey up the ladder.

'I see.' He leaned back in his chair, his eyes narrowing as he watched her. 'Well, you obviously have *some* experience—'

'You sound surprised!' she observed.

He ignored that. 'And we're going to need to establish the full extent of the embezzlement. Obviously. And then evolve some kind of strategy to resolve it. Aren't we, Kiloran?'

Despite her good intentions to remain cool and professional, Kiloran found it hard not to squirm beneath that grey-eyed scrutiny. It didn't help that he was making her feel incompetent, and neither did it help that he was so overpoweringly attractive.

He was making her aware of herself in a way which was quite alien to her. Since when had her breasts begun to ache and tingle just because some man's eyes had flickered over them in casual assessment? And why was she suddenly and acutely conscious that, beneath her dress, she had nothing covering her bottom other than a tiny and ridiculously insubstantial thong?

Her pulse beat strong and heavy, like a dull hammer at her wrists and temple. 'Wh-what do you want to know?' she asked from between parched lips, wondering if he had this effect on everyone.

'You can help me by giving me a few salient facts.'

'Like what?'

'Tell me about Eddie Peterhouse. How long he worked for Lacey's—general stuff.'

'He'd been with the company five years—'

His eyes bored into her. 'And you joined—when?'

'Two years ago.'

Adam gave a humourless smile. 'Which was around about the time the theft started.'

The accusation buzzed unsaid in the air around them. 'What are you implying?' she said shakily.

He didn't answer, not straight away. Let her work out the implication for herself. 'What did he look like?'

She narrowed her eyes at him in bemusement and gave her head a little shake. 'What's that got to do with anything?'

The movement meant that he could see the tight

thrust of her nipples pushing against the thin green silk, and the erotic thoughts which came tumbling into his head made it hard to concentrate. Hard being the operative word, he acknowledged grimly as he felt his body react to her unmistakable beauty. He didn't like this. He didn't like this one little bit. He shifted in his chair.

'The police will want a description—'

'But you're not the police,' she objected.

'Are you going to answer my question or not, Kiloran?' he snapped, and the grey eyes glittered like a winter sea. 'I asked you what he looked like.'

Bizarrely, she felt like throwing something at him and waltzing straight out of the boardroom, as if she were some reactive, emotional child. But she was not a child, and she did not have the luxury of being able to act on her emotions. She took a deep, steadying breath instead.

'He was tall.'

'You could be a little more specific than that?' he drawled. 'How tall?'

To her absolute horror, she heard herself saying, 'Not as tall as you.'

He gave a cynical smile. 'Not many men are,' he said, matter-of-factly. 'Again, specifics might be a little bit more helpful.'

She ran her tongue over her lips. 'Just over six feet, I guess.' He was still waiting. 'Fair hair. Blue eyes...' Her voice tailed off.

'Go on,' he urged obscurely. 'Was he in good shape?'

She only just prevented herself from saying, Not compared to you, but thank God she bit *that* back in time. Instead, she shrugged, as if she hadn't given it much thought at all—which in truth she hadn't. 'He was okay. He drank a little too much beer, but a lot of men do.'

'Did you find him attractive, Kiloran?'

She stared at him. '*What* did you say?'

'You heard. Did you?'

'No, of course I didn't! Why on earth should you ask me something as outrageous and insulting as that?'

'There's no "of course" about it,' he stated flatly. 'And neither is it outrageous or insulting. Human nature is very predictable and it's a classic scenario, I'm afraid. A man flatters a woman into thinking he's in love with her. And suddenly she's putty in his hands. Is that what happened, Kiloran? Did he seduce you? Ply you with pretty words and compliments? Maybe even take you to bed? Were you willing to put everything in his hands without bothering to check it out? Because that's what sometimes happens when a woman is in thrall of her lover.'

The crude way in which he was talking was having the most disastrous consequences. She could feel her palms growing wet and sticky as he purred out things like 'take you to his bed'. Was that why her heart was racing, because she was imagining *him* taking her to bed? She got to her feet and deliberately looked right down her nose at him. 'I don't have to listen to another word of this!'

'Sit down!'

'No, I won't sit down!' She stayed standing, the position of being able to look down on him giving her a brief feeling of superiority. 'Does my grandfather know the kind of interrogation you're subjecting me to?' she demanded coolly. 'Do you think he would stand for it?'

'Go ahead—ask him.' He shrugged.

'I don't think you'd like that for a moment, Mr Black. He'd have you out of here so fast you'd—'

'I don't think so,' he interrupted icily. 'He gave me a free rein and I intend using it.' But his words conjured up uncomfortably provocative images involving Kiloran on horseback, wearing a tight pair of jodhpurs, and he pushed them away with an almighty effort. 'I need to know whether you let your emotions cloud your judgement, that's all, Kiloran.'

She was about to blurt out that she never let emotions cloud her judgement, until she realised that she would be completely contradicting herself. She didn't blurt. She didn't react. She was calm and cool—so what the hell was happening to her? Quite the opposite. From the moment he had walked in here she had done nothing *but* react. To *him*. And it was time she stopped.

She sat down again, all the fire taken out of her, sucking in a deep breath and hoping it would steady her racing heart. 'For your information, no—I did not find him attractive.'

'Charming?'

'He was not without charm, no,' she admitted carefully.

'Good-looking?'

He was being so persistent! Eddie Peterhouse had regular features and had dressed in handmade Italian clothes, cleverly cut to disguise the slight swell of his beer-belly, but compared to Adam Black... 'Not particularly.'

He twisted a slim gold pen between long, slim fingers. 'So what would you say was the most overriding characteristic he possessed?'

She wanted to be truthful, even though her instincts baulked at having to tell this man *anything*! 'He seemed to know what he was doing. He exuded confidence.'

That figured. 'Con men always do. That's why people believe their lies and their evasion.'

'Do you put everyone in a snug little compartment?'

'Human nature being what it is, I usually find it works.'

How cold he sounded—more like a computer than a man. She wondered what compartment he had put *her* in, and then decided she would rather not think about it.

She gave him what she hoped was a calm and pleasant smile. 'Isn't wondering just why it all happened a bit of a waste of time?' she queried. 'What's done is done—surely what we need to do now is to rectify it?'

At last, he thought. A little common sense instead of the impenetrable maze of feminine logic! 'Yes.' The gleam from his grey eyes was one of challenge. 'Think you're up to it, Kiloran? It's going to be a lot of hard work.'

'I've never shirked from hard work.'

Looking at her, he doubted it. She looked as if nothing had troubled her more in her life than what moisturiser to use on that porcelain skin of hers. Or which item of clothing she was going to cover that delectable body with. 'I'm pleased to hear it. And the sooner we get started the better. I'll be back first thing on Monday morning.'

He began to collect the papers which lay on the desk in front of him, signalling, thought Kiloran, that the interview was at an end! He had grilled her, while she was left feeling as though she knew precisely nothing about the man who would now effectively be her boss! Just who *was* Adam Black?

'You come from round here, don't you?' she asked casually.

In the act of putting the papers into his briefcase, Adam paused, his eyes narrowing.

'That's right.' He wondered how much she knew and how much her grandfather had told her. And then asked himself did he really care what a spoilt little rich girl thought about him?

'Have you still got family living locally?' Kiloran persisted.

'Not any more,' he answered, but there was mockery in his eyes now as he enjoyed her feeling of powerlessness—that the man who would temporarily be calling the shots could just please himself. He gave a quick glance at his watch. 'I'm afraid I really do have to move.'

Leaving Kiloran feeling like someone with nowhere to go. She watched as he ran his fingers through his thick, dark hair and gave her a swift and not particularly friendly smile.

'I'll see you first thing on Monday,' he said. 'Goodbye, Kiloran.'

CHAPTER FOUR

WITH icy politeness, Kiloran showed Adam out, watching as his powerful car shot off down the long, winding drive, spraying gravel in its wake. Like a bat out of hell, she thought as the car became a pinprick in the distance, and then she went to look for her grandfather.

She found him in the library, and he looked up from his book as she burst in.

'Kiloran.' He smiled, but his eyes were wary.

'Grandfather, how *could* you?'

'How could I what, my dear?'

'Ask that…that…high-handed megalomaniac for help!'

'He might be high-handed,' he conceded, 'but he's no megalomaniac. Men like Adam Black don't have delusions of grandeur—they don't need to. His success speaks for itself. We're very lucky to have him.'

Lucky? It didn't feel lucky—it felt like… Kiloran couldn't define exactly how it did feel, but all she knew was that he had stirred her up into a state where she would have liked to have smashed something. She remembered his cool, dark good looks. His censorious face as he had taken her to task about her mismanagement!

Can't you face the simple truth, Kiloran? a voice

mocked her. Or is it that you simply can't bear the fact that you had to hear it from *him*?

'Well, if he's so wonderful—then why is he here? There must be a million other places he could be giving the benefit of his superior knowledge to!'

'He's doing me a favour,' said Vaughn slowly.

'Why?'

Her grandfather looked at her. 'That's the way it goes in business sometimes.'

Something in his voice was warning her off, and for the first time in her life Kiloran felt excluded, as if she were trying to dip her toe into a man's world, which she had no right to enter. And something in her grandfather's eyes told her not to bother trying.

'Relax, Kiloran,' said the old man gently. 'We couldn't be in better hands.'

How that phrase mocked her—and not just mocked her, but filled her with a strange kind of excitement as her mind was dazzled with disturbingly sensual images of being in Adam's hands. Of his experienced fingers playing sensual havoc all over her. And that was all part of the problem, she realised.

He wasn't the kind of man you could look upon with any kind of indifference. He dominated the space around him with such intensity that he seemed to leave a great, gaping hole in the atmosphere when he was gone. And how on earth was she going to co-operate with him and give of her best if all she could think about was how infuriatingly gorgeous he was?

Just stop it, she told herself fiercely.

Stop it.

Was that one of the reasons behind his success? That formidable presence? She remembered the way his face had become shuttered when she had asked if he still had family living close by. What really did she know about Adam Black, besides his successful professional reputation?

Nothing, that was what, and her grandfather obviously wasn't going to tell her anything either.

The party she was going to that night suddenly lost some of its allure. A fact borne out by the evening itself, when a perfectly acceptable man—who might normally have made a pleasant companion for the evening—left her feeling something she hadn't felt for a long time.

Restless.

Too restless to sleep. As if something had been woken in her that she could not put a name to, something which taunted her from the edge of her dreams, only to disappear when she opened her eyes. She tossed and turned into the small hours, drifting off only to wake up and find that it was still dark. And when she went down to breakfast, it was with an almighty headache.

She pushed the food around her plate like someone convalescing from an illness. She had known that things were bad, but somehow Adam Black's terse and critical assessment had made them seem a million times worse. Maybe rural living had blunted the edges of her judgement. Maybe her grandfather should never have appointed her in the first place.

Racked with self-doubt, she stared out at the summer garden—at the splashed colour spectrum of the roses and the bright blue spears of delphinium. What else could match a view like that? Certainly nothing that London could offer.

She had come back to live in the country for everything that view represented—a pace of life which was so much more relaxed than the hurly-burly of the city. Here, values seemed more grounded and there was time to do the things she enjoyed. Simple pleasures, far removed from the smoke-filled clatter of City bars. She rode her horse, played tennis and mixed with a set of people with similar tastes and passions.

No, maybe passion was the wrong word. Passion meant strong and uncontrollable emotion and Kiloran could certainly never have been accused of *that*.

Hers had been an uncertain childhood and her mother's moods capricious as she had sought happiness in the arms of a series of men until she had finally hit the jackpot and married her millionaire. Kiloran, in contrast, had strived for nothing more ambitious than balance, vowing never to go the way of her mother and look for happiness in someone else. She would find it within herself. She wanted nothing more than safety and security. Of knowing that she could survive on her own.

But a life which had seemed safe and predictable now looked anything but, and not just because the business was threatened. No, Adam Black had stormed into her life like a rampaging hurricane and, just like land left in the wake of a hurricane, she now felt distinctly flattened.

And distinctly disorientated.

In his London apartment, Adam stood beneath the jets of the shower and rubbed soap into his long, tanned legs, feeling the water beating warm and strong against him as it cascaded over his hair-roughened skin. He had been trying to wash away the memory of Kiloran Lacey and her pink and white beauty, telling himself that an unwilling sexual attraction was no basis for a close working relationship with the woman. But what choice did he have? He hadn't been *expecting* to be bowled over by that cool, insouciant air—it had just hit him out of the blue.

It hadn't happened like that for a long time—actually, never quite like *that* before—and never with anyone he worked with. She was off limits, he told himself. Strictly off limits.

He rubbed soap into firm, hard muscles but the physical contact only awakened feelings he would prefer to be subdued and, abruptly, he terminated the shower and roughly towelled himself dry. He slung on a pair of jeans and a T-shirt and flicked the message button on his answering machine, where the message light flashed the number eight onto the small screen.

Eight messages. He frowned. Had he really given his number out to that many people or had word just got around? He had only been back in England a month and yet already it seemed that he was in demand as the 'must-have' guest at every party. Single men were as rare as virgins, he thought wryly.

But he was tempted by none of the invitations on

offer as the machine beeped and whirred its way through the tape. He didn't want to be teamed up with a gorgeous accessory of a woman who would look at him and his lifestyle and wonder why he wasn't married and immediately set about righting that.

Nor have to fend off the attentions of the hostess who was invariably feeling jaded with marriage and on the lookout for a quick fix of sexual excitement.

And it seemed that dissatisfaction went hand in hand with affluence. Once, affluence had seemed like the answer to everything, but maybe that was because when you didn't have something you strove and strove until you did. Or, at least, he did. And then when you got it—what then?

Another challenge, he guessed. Something like Lacey's. A little, old-fashioned ship, bobbing around on the pirate-infested sea of big business.

He gave a slow smile, enjoying the analogy, even if Kiloran Lacey somehow and distractingly got into the picture, tied to some mast with the waves plastering her clothes to her body.

He groaned as he felt the unwelcome throb of desire and, annoyed with himself, picked up the phone on the first ring instead of letting it go directly to the answering machine.

'Adam?' came a breathless, eager voice. 'It's Carolyn.'

It took a moment to fit the face to the voice and when he did, he nodded. She was beautiful and amusing enough to take to the theatre with him, surely? 'Carolyn,' he murmured. 'Good to hear you.'

*   *   *

While the Lacey factory lay on the outskirts of the small, nearby town, the administration block had been built by Kiloran's great-grandfather within the grounds of the mansion itself. He had been a man ahead of his time in more ways than one and he had wanted to see as much of his children growing up as possible.

Kiloran had always enjoyed the easy access between work and home, but when she walked into her office on Monday morning to find a horribly familiar figure sitting at *her* desk she felt as though she were being invaded on all fronts.

Long legs were stretched out in front of him, the soft fabric of his suit stretching over the hard muscle of his thighs, and she found herself thinking how broad his shoulders were when viewed from this angle.

The jet-dark head was lifted and the face which was raised to greet the sound of her entering could by no stretch of the imagination be described as welcoming, but that didn't stop her heart missing a beat.

Kiloran swallowed. 'Good morning, Adam,' she said carefully. 'What are you doing here?'

'What does it look like?' he questioned coolly. 'Working.' He gave a pointed look at the expensive gold timepiece which gleamed discreetly above an immaculate white cuff. 'What's this?' he questioned sardonically. 'Your half-day?'

She felt so unsettled at seeing him, particularly seeing him sitting looking so arrogantly territorial, that she immediately went on the defensive. 'It's nine o'clock,' she answered. 'The time when most normal people start working.'

He put down his pen with a clatter. 'These are not normal times, Kiloran,' he returned. 'I thought you realised that! And, besides, I'm always at my desk by seven-thirty.'

Well, bully for you, she thought. 'How did you get here?'

'I flew.'

'Seriously?'

He gave a click of irritation. 'Of course I didn't—the nearest airfield is miles away. That was what was known as irony, Kiloran.' Though he doubted whether she would know irony if it got up and performed a little dance for her. 'I drove.'

'This morning?'

'Very early this morning.'

It must have been virtually daybreak when he had started out—because even when the roads were empty, the journey still took two hours from London. That would probably account for the smudges of faint blue shadows beneath those magnificent eyes. Or had he spent his weekend engaged in pursuits which would guarantee a lack of sleep? Probably, if the newspapers were to be believed.

She felt at a loss. 'Would you like coffee?' she asked.

Silently, Adam counted to ten. 'No, Kiloran,' he said steadily. 'I would not like coffee. What I would like is for you to take the weight off those pretty feet and grab yourself a chair—'

'You're sitting in it,' she said stonily, bristling at the 'pretty feet' bit. 'This is my office, remember? My desk. And my chair.'

'And have you sorted a room out for me?'

'Not yet, no.'

He shook his head, as a teacher would to a child who had not presented their work on time. 'You knew I was coming—you've had two days to organise something.' He leaned back and studied her. 'So why haven't you?'

She couldn't ever remember being spoken to in such a way—not even in her very first job, when she had been the most junior of juniors. 'I'll do it straight away!'

'Not straight away, no. Here—' He gestured towards the swivel chair beside him. 'Come over here and sit down.'

She felt like Little Red Riding Hood being enticed by the big, bad wolf, but there was something so authoritative in his tone that she found herself doing exactly what he said.

'There,' he murmured, a glimmer of amusement sparking in the depths of the stormy eyes as she perched on the seat next to his, noting the awkward set of her shoulders and her frozen posture. She really didn't like him one bit, did she? he observed wryly. 'How's that?'

It was awful. Or rather, it wasn't. It was the opposite of awful. She could never remember being so aware of a man in her life. This close, she could catch traces of some subtle musky aftershave, which only drew her attention to the faint shadowing at his jaw. He must have shaved so early, she found herself thinking inconsequentially—and yet already the new growth was visible. The breath caught in her throat; she knew that it would be rude to look away from the grey eyes, and feared that if she did he would sense her discomfiture.

And realise the cause of it.

'Perfect,' she said lightly. 'But only as a very temporary measure.'

Yeah. He wasn't going to argue with her about *that*. This was more than a little too close for comfort, that was for sure. He tried to rationalise her appeal, just as he had been trying to rationalise it since the moment he had seen her again—telling himself that the woman he had spent Saturday evening with had been just as beautiful.

So what was it about Kiloran Lacey? What was so special about those green cat's eyes and the shiny blonde hair? Was her appeal strengthened simply because she *was* off limits?

He let his eyes drift over her. The simple summer dress she wore dropped in a floaty little hem to her knees. Sweet knees, he found himself thinking reluctantly. Her bare arms were strong and toned and lightly tanned and he found himself wondering if she was an exercise fanatic. Probably, he decided. It wouldn't surprise him if she had had her own high-tech gym installed somewhere in the bowels of this enormous house. An extravagance incurred at the expense of the company, no doubt, and his mouth flattened into a thin line of disapproval.

'Right.' With an effort he brought himself back to the subject in hand, drawing out a sheet of cream-coloured writing paper from the sheath of documents in front of him. 'Let's see what we have here.'

Kiloran took one brief glance at the distinctive, spidery handwriting and her heart sank.

'Recognise this?' he asked shortly.

She nodded. 'It's from my aunt Jacqueline.'

'It certainly is. But she's more than just your aunt, isn't she, Kiloran?' He saw her shift a little in her chair. 'She just happens to be the second biggest shareholder of Lacey's soaps and—'

'And let me guess—she's angry?'

'Angry?' Adam's dark lashes shielded his eyes as he lowered his glance to scan over the letter. 'To say that she is angry would be something of an understatement. And I have to say that I have some sympathy with her.'

Well, he would—wouldn't he? 'May I read it?'

'You won't like it.'

'Oh, I'm tough enough to take Aunt Jacqueline's...' But her voice tailed off as she began to read. Angry wasn't the word for it. The words seemed to sizzle off the page.

The letter didn't pull any punches. And there was a particularly wounding paragraph.

I have no wish to apportion blame, Vaughn.

Of course you don't, thought Kiloran wryly.

But nonetheless, someone must take responsibility for the theft. If Kiloran had had the courage to admit that she was out of her depth, then none of this might have happened and as a consequence, my financial security and that of my daughter might not now be threatened.

Kiloran read on.

I have been comforted by your news that Adam Black has been brought in and I must congratulate you on having hired a man of such formidable reputation.

Kiloran wondered fleetingly how Adam Black felt about having been described as 'hired'.

In fact, I should take some comfort in a meeting with him at the earliest possible opportunity, and I would be pleased if you could arrange this for me.

She put the letter down. 'Perhaps it would make everyone feel better if they just lined me up in the stocks and threw things at me—that's what they used to do in days gone by, isn't it?'

'Self-pity won't help, Kiloran.'

'No.' Is that what it had sounded like? Suddenly, the thought that this man might be judging her and finding her wanting was too much. Let him see that she wasn't going to crumple and go to pieces. She lifted her head and met the assessing gaze full-on. 'She wants to meet with you.'

'So I see. It's not a bad idea—put everyone in the picture. I'm going to arrange a meeting of all the major shareholders—'

'When?'

'Just as soon as we've made some headway.' There was a pointed silence before he continued. 'And we won't make any just so long as we sit around doing nothing.'

'Are you always such a hard taskmaster, Adam?' she questioned softly.

Adam's throat dried as the words came out like some sultry provocation, conjuring up an image which was uncomfortably erotic. Did she do that deliberately? he wondered. Was she aware that, when she said things like that, most red-blooded men would melt?

'Only if I need to be,' he answered silkily, trying to ignore the lush thrust of her breasts and the hint of lace behind the thin fabric of her dress. God, he couldn't stand a minute more of this than he had to! 'I want you to organise an office for me,' he shot out. 'I need e-mail, phone links and a fax machine.'

'I'll get one of the secretaries to do it.'

'Better had,' he agreed evenly. 'Because in the meantime I'm going to have to stay right here.'

If anything could be designed to make her act swiftly, it was the thought that this man would be intruding on *her* space for any longer than was absolutely necessary. The office, which by any standards was a large and spacious room, seemed suddenly to have constricted to the dimensions of a shoebox.

On legs which felt like cotton wool, Kiloran rose to her feet. 'I'll go and see to it straight away.'

'Thanks.'

He watched her graceful movement as she swayed out of the room, the pert line of her bottom thrusting with tantalising appeal against the floaty material of her dress, and wondered what kind of life she led outside the office. Wasn't she lonely, living out here in the back of beyond? Or was there a man who ran his fingers through the thick, shiny splendour of her hair in bed at night? There must be. A woman like that did not look as though she was born to be celibate for long.

A thoughtful look stayed on his face. He was puzzled at the progression of his thoughts and he did not like to be puzzled. Yet he had worked closely with beautiful women before, and not once had he wasted time thinking about what they did or didn't get up to in the bedroom.

His mouth flattened. There was a very good rule for not mixing business with pleasure, he remembered. It meant that you could keep your mind on the job. He picked up his pen and viciously began to underline various paragraphs on the page in front of him.

After a couple of minutes Kiloran came back into the office. 'Everyone's talking—I think the office staff ought to meet you.'

He looked up. 'Oh?'

'They know something isn't right and now there'll

be rumours circulating because some mystery man is demanding an office!'

'What do you want to tell them?'

'That you're our knight in shining armour?' Now what on earth had made her come out with something like *that*?

Bizarrely, the image pleased him and he gave a slow smile. 'Is that how you see me, then, Kiloran?'

She could have bitten her words back, but, stupidly enough, yes, it was. Childhood memory became fused with adult reality and the result was perplexing because the perception remained exactly the same. Yet he looked nothing like a storybook character. He was dressed in a beautiful charcoal suit, which provided the perfect backdrop for the glittering grey eyes, and he looked the personification of the modern executive.

But there was something about the steely determination which hardened the corners of the lush mouth and something about the shadowed jaw which meant that the clothes and the setting counted for nothing. Adam Black had the age-old looks and charisma of the conquering hero.

'Hardly,' she said lightly. 'You've forgotten your horse!'

He resisted a smile. 'I think we'll just tell the truth, shall we? That way there can be no misunderstanding.'

She nodded, her throat still dry. 'I'll go and call them in.'

Kiloran left the office hastily, before he had a chance to say anything else, or to look at her again with that coolly quizzical stare, which made her feel as if she'd never been looked at by a man before. And before he could see the colour which had made her cheeks feel as if they were on fire.

Now what was *that* all about? she asked herself as she headed for her secretary's office. No one was denying that he was potent and powerful and attractive, but she knew the dangers of men like that. Men who could just snap their fingers and any woman would go running straight into their arms. She liked gentle men—*gentlemen*—not men who looked as though they would drag you to their beds and then kick you out when they'd had their fill of you.

'Are you okay, Kiloran?' Heather, her secretary, was looking at her anxiously. 'You look like you've seen a ghost!'

Not a ghost, thought Kiloran grimly. Ghosts didn't exude so much sex appeal that it positively radiated off them. 'Come and meet our newest member of staff, Adam Black,' she said, forcing a smile.

'Is that the man who looks like a film star?' sighed Heather.

'Too rugged to be a film star,' said Kiloran automatically, before turning to her secretary in surprise. 'Have you met him, then?'

'No, but the cleaner did, first thing,' confided Heather. 'Said she thought she'd died and gone to heaven!'

More like hell, thought Kiloran, but she forced a smile.

'And then he *made her a cup of coffee*!'

Heather made it sound as though an angel had suddenly materialised and started boiling the kettle! 'Did he, now? Well, liberation is obviously alive and well and waiting in my office!'

'I'll go and get the others!'

The staff trailed in to meet him and Kiloran watched as Adam rose to his feet as if he owned the place, then graciously shook them each by the hand until he had them virtually eating out of his.

'I'm going to be very frank with you,' he said winningly, 'because I believe that honesty is the best policy.' He paused, looking around, his stormy eyes assessing their curious expressions. 'Most of you will know that Eddie Peterhouse has left the company, but what you will not know is that funds are missing and unaccountable for, and we would very much like to question him.'

There was an audible gasp and then a buzz of chatter.

He looked around the room and every voice fell silent. 'The police are looking for him, and we are co-operating in every way we can,' he said smoothly. 'Everything is in hand. I will be working here in collaboration with Kiloran until we get things back on their feet as quickly as possible. Until then, things will carry on as before—but in the meantime I will be at the helm. Is that understood?'

They all nodded, visibly captivated by his tough, no-nonsense air of determination.

'Good,' he said and treated them to a devastating smile. 'Well, that's all, then, unless anyone has any questions they'd like to put to me?'

No one did, he seemed to have said it all, and they filed out as obediently as lambs being sent off to slaughter. But once they had gone Kiloran turned to him, and, try as she might, she couldn't hide the shaking hurt in her voice. 'Did that make you feel better?'

He didn't react to the green fire sparking from her eyes. 'What?'

'Telling them about the missing funds!'

'Like I said,' he drawled, 'I believe that honesty is the best policy.'

'And then virtually conducting a coup right in front of me! You really put me in my place, didn't you, Adam? "I will be at the helm!" Does it give you pleasure to always be in the driving seat?' She wished she hadn't said it, and as soon as the words were out of her mouth she regretted them, for they took on an unmistakably sensual undertone, and, from the darkening of his eyes, the fact had not escaped him either.

'That's the way it goes, Kiloran. That's what was agreed with Vaughn.' He fixed her with an impatient air. 'There's no room for egos at a time like this. Once I've gone, you can play Managing Director to your heart's content.'

She opened her mouth to reply and then shut it

again, for what could she say which wouldn't make things degenerate into a shouting match?

He gestured to the pile of papers. 'And now, if you've quite finished discussing office hierarchy,' he said sardonically, 'we've got work to do.'

CHAPTER FIVE

ADAM worked like a demon.

All morning long he crunched numbers, building financial models on Kiloran's computer while the fax machine worked overtime. His single-mindedness was impressive, and Kiloran sat beside him, trying not to stare at the way his hair waved thickly around his ear and to concentrate on answering the series of questions he shot at her so rapidly that she felt as if she were taking part in a televised quiz show.

During the morning his jacket came off. Then the tie. A little later the top two buttons of his shirt were impatiently opened and Kiloran observed these with a horrified kind of fascination. What next? she thought. Would he start peeling off his trousers? Would he soon be sitting there wearing nothing but a pair of—undoubtedly—silk boxer shorts?

He looked up and frowned. 'Is something the matter, Kiloran? You're looking quite flushed.'

'It's…hot in here,' she managed.

'Yeah. It is—why don't you open the other window?'

She was surprised he didn't tack on *like a good girl*, but she was glad of the excuse to turn away and to allow the summer air to wash over her heated cheeks. She prayed that he couldn't read her mind as she turned back to pick up a sheaf of papers and begin to work through them.

At one point, Heather poked her head round the door. 'The canteen's closing soon,' she announced. 'And they want to know are you eating lunch?'

He didn't even look up. 'Get them to send some sandwiches and coffee over, would you, Heather?'

Heather raised her eyebrows expressively in Kiloran's direction as if to say, *Tyrant.* 'Sandwiches all right for you?'

'Fine,' said Kiloran shortly, and got to her feet as Heather disappeared. 'But if I don't get some fresh air soon, I'll expire. I'm going to take a walk in the garden, if that's all right with you, Adam?'

He looked up then, saw the strained expression on her face and wondered if he had been working her too hard. She lifted her hand to push away a stray strand of blonde hair and her wrists, he noted inconsequentially, were tiny, as delicate as the slender ankles. *She* looked delicate. So delicate she might break. He gave a frowning glance at his watch. And it was getting on for two o'clock—they had worked right through without a single break.

He rubbed his eyes. 'Sure.' He removed his hand from the mouse, stretched, and yawned. 'I might come with you—you can give me a guided tour of the grounds.' His voice deepened. 'Show me your beautiful garden, Kiloran.'

The soft tone momentarily disarmed her even more than the yawn, which gave her a glimpse of a rare moment of relaxation. Did he always drive himself so hard, she wondered, and if so—why?

She smiled. 'Is that an order?'

'Mmm.' It was, he realised, the first time she had really smiled at him. She should do it more often. Definitely. But there again, maybe she shouldn't. Not if he wanted to stay sane. 'Come on.'

She led him outside and Adam stood, momentarily dazzled by the bright light, thinking that the garden seemed too humble a word to describe the sprawling Lacey grounds which surrounded the grand, old mansion. He felt as though he had stepped into an exotic paradise where brightly coloured blooms dazzled in the flowerbeds and perfect lawns were broken only by trees and shrubs. There was a sense of permanence and of timelessness which seemed to seep into his senses and for a moment he almost envied her.

'It's beautiful,' he said slowly.

'Yes.' She looked around her, and contentment stole over her. 'It is.'

'I've never seen some of these flowers before.'

'Probably not. A lot of them are extremely rare.'

'Who planted them?'

'My great-great-grandfather. He lived in India for the early part of his life and, when he came home, he brought back all the shrubs and trees and flowers he could. We had hothouses specially built. Some of the plants failed, but some of them flourished. The flowers were used to make the basic scent for the soaps, and the rest you know.'

She watched for some kind of reaction, but the

sculpted profile remained as unmoving as if it had been carved from rare black marble. For a moment she saw it through *his* eyes.

'It's more than just a business, you know, Adam,' she said suddenly. 'It's a way of life. It *is* a life. *Our* life. The way that Laceys have always lived.' Unconsciously, her voice took on a low conviction. 'Can't you understand why it's so important that we don't lose it all?'

He began to walk towards a confection of water, shaded by trees, so that the sunlight dappled and glinted on the surface. She had something he never would have, he realised—not if he became the most powerful man in the universe. A sense of continuity, of generations going back as well as the generations who were yet to come. And through it all the house remained, solid and enduring—a symbol of past and present and future.

He watched as Kiloran walked over to join him. The sun was behind her, shining through her, so that she looked like someone caught in a spotlight. The brightness haloed her hair with a golden shimmer and outlined the lush, young body beneath the summer dress she wore. She looked exquisite—like a goddess, with the world at her feet—and hadn't that always been the way of it?

She took it all for granted, this beautiful woman to whom the gods had been so generous. And what would she be without all these trappings? he wondered. Would she still have that tantalisingly aristocratic air about her?

His mouth curved with disdain. 'God, Kiloran—is that all you can think about?' he demanded. 'Your family? And your family's position in society, as land-owners and employers?'

'But that's just the whole point,' she appealed.

'What—status?' he snapped back.

'It's nothing to do with status! People round here rely on us for jobs—they always have done! Why, you did yourself—once.'

Adam felt his nerve-endings tingle. So she wanted his gratitude, did she? Was he supposed to fall to his knees in front of her? 'Oh, your arrogance and your pride, Kiloran,' he said softly. 'Are you seeking to put me in my place? Or simply to remind me of your position of ownership?'

'You make me sound like a snob,' she said bitterly.

'And you're not?'

'No! Never!'

'Do you know why your grandfather gave me a job?'

'No.'

'He hasn't told you?'

She shook her head. 'He refused.'

So she had asked, had she?

He hadn't intended to tell her, but suddenly it be-came important that he did. Just how important was her position in society to her? he wondered. She had denied being a snob—well, let him see the evidence for himself.

'I come from a single-parent family,' he said, star-

ing out to where a cypress tree had darkened the lawn
with its shadow.

'Well, so, as a matter of fact, do I!'

'It's not quite the same. Your mother was a widow.'
He nearly said 'respectable' because that was usually
the word associated with widows, but Kiloran's
mother had in no way been respectable. 'Mine didn't
even know who my father was.' He said the words
matter-of-factly. *'He could have been one of many.'*

She returned his gaze steadily. 'I see.'

He had been watching her face for shock, or some
kind of condemnation, but there was nothing but a
calm acceptance and perversely he *wanted* shock.
Wanted condemnation. He wanted her to judge him
and find him wanting, for then—couldn't he do the
same with her? Wouldn't it make life a hell of a lot
easier if he could imagine her like her mother—with
her mother's shallow values? Instead of those emerald-
bright eyes gazing up at him and threatening to melt
him with their understanding green fire.

'I grew up in Barton Street—do you know it?'

'I know *of* it—I've never been there.'

'No,' he said shortly. 'I don't imagine that you
would.' He watched as a bird splashed around in the
water. 'My childhood was spent with a succession of
"uncles" filing through the house.'

He spoke as if he were reciting share prices, as if
he didn't care. Was his heart as hard as his face suggested? 'That must have been—awful.'

He looked at her. It probably sounded as if he were
describing life on Mars to her. 'Awful? Yeah—you

could say that. It became harder to tolerate as I grew older. But I had a way out. I was good at school and I worked hard. I worked hard at my Saturday job, too. I used to work at the baker's, in town. Know it?'

'Of course.'

He had never told anyone this, he realised. He had suppressed it for years. So was it being back here that made it all bubble to the surface again? And why *her*?

'I'd saved my wages ever since I'd started,' he said. 'I knew I was going to need every penny I had to help get me through college.'

Kiloran watched him. 'What happened?'

'I had the key to the bakery because I used to work some nights.' There was a pause. Long and heavy and pregnant. 'One night my mother's lover stole it. He broke in and he ransacked the place. Took everything there was to take—including a till full of money. The following morning they had both gone.'

'Your mother, too?' she breathed, aghast.

'That's right.'

'What happened?'

'They sacked me. Of course. Threatened to go to the police unless the money was paid back. Yet how could I get a job to pay it back when people thought I was dishonest? That's when Vaughn stepped in.' His eyes were very bright and very hard. 'Do you see now the debt I owe him—that he trusted me when no one else would give me a chance?'

Kiloran nodded, shaken by what he had told her. 'And your mother? Do you still see her?'

'I never saw her again,' he said flatly. At first he

had had no desire to—her betrayal not seeming to warrant it. And as time had gone by he had buried it; it had seemed easier all round to do that. Besides, he had a high-enough public profile—shouldn't she have come to *him* after everything that had happened? 'So how does that make you feel now, Kiloran? Powerful?'

'Powerful?' She shook her head. 'Why should I? None of us have any control over the circumstances in which we were brought up.' She bit her lip as she remembered her mother's indiscretions—the way she had blocked them out. Ignoring them and hoping that they might go away. It had taken her mother's marriage for her to eventually start behaving like a grown-up. 'And anyway, as you have just pointed out—if there's any position of authority at the moment, then it's yours. You're the one calling the shots!'

Her words made him focus on the now, rather than on the then. 'Do you really think that the success of small industries such as yours are set in stone?' he questioned gently. 'It isn't your God-given right to own all this and to oversee it. Society is about flux and change as much as stability. And people have to adapt to the times.'

'You're saying it's hopeless, is that it?'

He shook his dark head, her dark, haunted eyes stabbing remorselessly at his conscience. Why was he doing this? Was he unconsciously trying to punish her because she made him want her more than he was comfortable with? Or maybe for having the roots he lacked? And if that was the case, then he was being neither honest, nor fair.

'I'm not saying it's hopeless. If I thought that, then I wouldn't be wasting my time here, would I?'

'Thanks,' she said drily.

'You're going to have to learn to start listening to the truth, Kiloran,' he said roughly. 'And the truth is that I don't have any answers for you, not yet. The company might be salvageable; it might not—and until I have every available fact and figure in front of me, we can't possibly know that.'

'And if I'd been keener, more alert—then I'd have spotted Eddie's deception and everything would have been just perfect, is that it?'

He turned to face her. 'I can't answer that either,' he said honestly.

'You mean it might have been?'

'You don't need me to tell you that.'

'Oh, God!' She turned away, hugging her arms to her chest as if she were standing there in the dead of winter instead of on a bright, summer's day. 'What have I done?'

He heard in her voice the hopelessness he had once felt himself, and a feeling like that was never forgotten, so that empathy reared an unexpected head. 'Kiloran—'

She turned back, and all she could see were the hard planes of his face, the sunlight casting shadows over his features, his eyes glitteringly bright as he stared down at her. 'What?'

'Let's just see how it goes, shall we?'

She nodded, biting on her lip and hoping he didn't notice the hint of tears which threatened to spring up at the back of her eyes. For a moment, neither of them moved and Kiloran felt the slow burn of unwanted desire.

Because the frustration at the situation she found herself in was bubbling up into another kind of frustration. She had never felt this way about a man and never before had she wanted so much for someone to take her in his arms and blot it all out.

He gazed down at her, the message in her eyes unmistakable, and Adam was too experienced in the ways of women not to have read it correctly.

She wanted him.

Her softening lips told him, as did the darkening of her eyes. He didn't need to glance down towards her breasts to know that their buds would be exquisitely tight, longing for the teasing caress of his fingers or his lips. And they were alone…not a soul would know…

She wanted him, and for a moment he was more than tempted. To tumble her down onto the soft grass and to tangle his fingers in the silk of her hair.

But he moved away from her.

'Come on. We'd better go and eat lunch,' he said abruptly, and willed the dark hunger of longing to leave him in peace.

It was gone eight when he finally switched the computer off and looked at her, and Kiloran had been wondering whether he intended working right through the night.

'Had enough?' he asked.

More than enough—but she gave him what she hoped was a coping smile. 'Sure.'

He rose to his feet, towering over her like some dark, avenging angel. 'Then I'll be going. I have to drive back to London.'

It seemed stupid not to say it—if it had been anyone else she would have said it. 'It's a long drive after a hard day. Do you—do you want a bed for the night?'

His senses sprang into life and just for a moment he allowed himself the fantasy. She wasn't offering *her* bed, but that didn't stop him imagining it. In his mind, he laid her down on a big bed, then slowly drew off the green dress, picturing the lush perfection of her body clothed in nothing but silk and lace. The secret curves and shadows hidden by outrageous items of underwear. He would not remove them, not at first. He would allow his eyes to feast before his lips and his fingers and...

'I don't think that's such a good idea, do you?' he questioned softly.

'I guess not,' she agreed, but she didn't ask him why, and the air was tight with a tension so tight that she felt she could snap it.

CHAPTER SIX

'I'VE arranged a meeting of the shareholders,' Adam announced as Kiloran came into his office with her arms full of files.

She put the files down on his desk. 'When?'

'A week next Sunday in London seems to be the only time we can get everyone together at such short notice. I've arranged to use my new offices,' he said, leaning back in his chair and narrowing his eyes. 'That okay with you, Kiloran?'

What could she say? That she would prefer to be out riding her horse rather than having to endure a grilling by the shareholders? And why was he glowering at her like that—hadn't she been sweetness and light all day? All week? 'Sunday's fine.'

And he now had all the figures at his disposal, thank heavens. The end was in sight, though he knew that he was going to miss the sight of *her*. Maybe even miss her feisty little ways and that occasional stubborn pout. He ran his fingers through his thick dark hair. 'I think we're in business.' He yawned. 'Do you want to hear my recommendations?'

'Better had.'

She drew up a chair—one delicious thigh resting uncomfortably close to his. Surreptitiously, he shifted his leg away. 'It's exactly as I first suspected—you're lagging way behind the times. You need to take a serious look at your overheads—and I'm not talking about production here.'

She raised her eyebrows. 'Meaning?'

He glanced down at the wad of papers. 'For example, hiring a part-time designer would be a lot more cost-effective than using expensive design agencies as you are at the moment.'

Kiloran nodded. It made sense. Such simple sense that she wondered why she'd never thought of it herself. Had she been guilty of burying her head in the sand?

'But that will increase my wage bill,' she said, biting her lip.

He saw her stricken face. 'Yes—but you've got enough work so it will be cheaper in the long run,' he said gently.

'Yes.' She looked at him steadily. 'Anything else?'

'You could sell some of your own shares. Plough some of the proceeds back.'

Kiloran nodded. 'Okay.'

He had expected to have to fight her on this and her easy agreement uncharacteristically took the wind right out of his sails. 'You know, you've done many good things—'

'Thanks,' she said drily.

'No, I mean it—the way you've kept abreast of trends—diversifying into the aromatherapy line and the scented candles.'

His praise meant more to her than it should have done, but they weren't sitting here with the intention of boosting her ego. They were here to seek solutions. 'Anything else?'

His face grew closed. 'Well, yes. The way you live will really have to be curtailed if you want Lacey's to carry on.'

'Curtailed?' She narrowed her eyes. 'What's that supposed to mean?'

'Just that the business is helping fund a self-indulgent lifestyle.'

'Self-indulgent?' She spat the words out indignantly.

'Sure. You rattle around in that great big house—'

'If you're even thinking I'd agree to sell it, Adam, then think again—Grandfather would never agree to—'

'Let me finish,' he said coolly. 'I said nothing about selling, did I? I know how much it means to you—but you could think about utilising the space. Letting out some of the bigger rooms for conferences can be lucrative.'

'Make the house into a kind of business, is that what you're saying?'

He ignored the squeak of horror in her voice. 'Lots of people have to do it. Or maybe you consider yourself too special to deign to try?'

That hurt. 'Is that what you think?'

He shrugged. 'You don't seem very willing.'

'Well, you can hardly expect me to embrace the suggestion with whoops of joy. And it would take a lot of organisation.'

'But it can be done.' He cradled his dark head in

the palms of his hands as he watched her from be-tween narrowed eyes. 'As for the cash flow problem, which needs to be solved in the interim—' he paused, anticipating her reaction to *this* '—you could sell one of your paintings. That Augustus John etching you've got hanging in the boardroom is very saleable.'

'I didn't know you knew we *had* an Augustus John.'

'Or just surprised that I recognised it?' he queried sardonically.

Their eyes met and he saw the colour rise in her cheeks.

'Are you serious?' she demanded.

'For heaven's sake, Kiloran,' he said impatiently. 'You've got loads of pictures hanging around the house. Surely you can lose one of them?'

'You make it sound like they're posters you buy in the local art shop!' she protested. 'Don't you realise that—?'

'If you're going to start telling me that you've had them since for ever and that they are very special to you, then please don't bother,' he retorted. 'I'm not so dense that I can't see that—but you asked for a solution to your problems and I'm coming up with a fairly painless one.'

'*Painless?*' Selling her shares she could cope with—but the etching was part of her past, her life. It symbolised something that was deeply important to her and yet Adam Black was dismissing it in a single word.

'You've got a better idea? Then please do enlighten me,' he snapped, and then, with an effort, levelled out his voice. 'Listen, Kiloran—you put a highly saleable painting on the market and you walk into the share-holders' meeting with that knowledge. Money in the bank, end of story. They'll be full of questions but you've got your answer all ready. Takes all the angst away. Simple.'

Simple? 'And there's really no other way?'

'You tell me.'

She felt like telling him that it felt as though he were tearing her life apart, shred by excruciating shred, but he was only there as an impartial arbitrator, after all. How could he be expected to feel passion-ately about an inanimate object he was not connected to? She wondered if he felt passionately about anything.

'I guess I have no choice.'

But he shook his head. 'Oh, yes—there's always a choice.' He was losing his patience now. 'You could choose not to take my advice and watch the company fold—but if you think some damned etching is worth all that, then go ahead. Keep it!'

Slowly she raised her head and met the assessing grey stare. 'Very well, I'm happy to sell it—but I'll have to get my grandfather's approval,' she said flatly.

Briefly, he wondered if he was being a little too Draconian—but what other way was there? She was fighting to hold onto a lifestyle she could no longer afford, and she was stubborn—even her grandfather had told him that. And stubborn women were like horses—you had to work them hard to make them realise who was boss.

He expelled a breath. 'Good. The other thing which might interest you is that my job is done now, and that after the meeting of the shareholders you need never see me again.' He allowed a smile to linger. 'I know how much that will please you, Kiloran.'

It should have done, it really should. But unfortunately, you didn't always feel the way you were supposed to. Why was she filled with a sinking certainty that Lacey's was going to seem a very dull place without Adam Black? 'Best piece of news I've had all week,' she agreed blandly.

And hoped that the lie didn't show.

CHAPTER SEVEN

THE meeting of the shareholders was held in Adam's prestigious new offices close to Fenchurch Street station in the middle of the hustle and bustle of the City, set right in the middle of the capital's most high-powered heartland.

Kiloran found the offices easily enough and a uniformed security guard let her into the towering building, where a vast marble foyer glittered beneath the deflected light of crystal chandeliers.

'Take the lift to the thirtieth floor, miss.' He smiled.

The lift mimicked the feeling in her stomach as it rose smoothly to the top of the building, and when Kiloran stepped out she followed the low hum of voices which drifted out from an open-doored room. As she walked in, ten faces turned to look at her, eight male and two female.

But the face she noticed above all the others belonged, predictably, to Adam. He sat with his tie loosened, his black hair ruffled and the grey eyes glittering with an intensity which made the chandeliers seem muted in comparison.

It had been little over a week since she'd seen him yet her heart began to hammer hard and strong beneath her suddenly heavy, aching breasts. As if his physical presence had set up some clamouring interior recognition which lit a touch-paper to her senses.

He looked up, unsurprised by the rush of pleasure at seeing her standing there. She would make any man with a pulse feel like that, he reasoned. 'Kiloran,' he said evenly. 'Good. Everyone else is here.'

'Waiting,' said the woman beside him, with a rather pointed little smile.

Jacqueline was Kiloran's aunt, pretty and blonde and very like her mother to look at—with what looked like the entire contents of a cosmetics counter applied to her face.

'Hello, Aunt Jacqueline,' said Kiloran.

'You're looking a bit peaky, dear,' said her aunt, with a brittle smile, as she held a pale cheek up for a kiss. 'Been dieting?'

Having Adam Black around had made food seem like a necessary evil, but she certainly wasn't going to say *that*! 'Not intentionally.' She smiled.

'Come and sit down,' said Adam, pointing to the one empty space, directly opposite his.

And then Kiloran noticed who had claimed the other seat beside him. It was her cousin, Julia—as dark as her mother was blonde—and very, very beautiful, in a sloe-eyed, Madonna type of way. She was dressed expensively in a scarlet dress, and her raven hair fell in two gleaming wings on either side of her face. She was also, Kiloran noted, staring at Adam and looking as smug as a cat who had just found an unexpected saucer of cream and had decided to keep it all to herself. She couldn't blame her.

'Hi, Jules.'

Julia tore her eyes away from Adam and gave her cousin a conspiratorial grin. 'Oh, hi, Kiloran.'

They hadn't seen each other for getting on for a year, not since Julia's last birthday party—always a lavish affair—which Kiloran sometimes suspected that she was invited to mainly to admire the showcase of her glamorous London life.

'This is an amazing place, isn't it?' asked Julia, glancing around at the ornate, high-ceilinged room. 'Makes Lacey's look like a doll's house!'

'It's certainly impressive,' said Kiloran drily.

Julia picked up the silver pot which stood in front of her, as if she were the hostess at a coffee morning. 'Can I get anyone a coffee? How about you, Adam? You look as if you could use one.'

He shook his head, watching Kiloran as she sat down and smoothed back her hair, so that it looked as if she were wearing a sleek, blonde cap. She had faint blue shadows beneath her eyes and he wondered if she had been spending sleepless nights. You and me both, honey, he thought grimly.

'No, thanks,' he said shortly. 'There's no point in hanging around and, now that Kiloran's here, I think we just ought to crack on with things.' He paused and then raised his voice, so that everyone stopped chatting and looked at him. 'The first thing I want to say is that the situation is not quite as gloomy as it could be—'

'Really?' Aunt Jacqueline raised her eyebrows disbelievingly. 'You mean that the missing money has been returned?'

Adam gave a patient smile. 'Unfortunately, no. But we *do* have a contingency plan.'

'Really?' said Jacqueline again.

'I have already made recommendations to Kiloran, which she has agreed to implement.'

The grey eyes met hers in a questioning look, which she answered with an imperceptible nod, and every face in the room was turned curiously towards her.

'These involve the letting-out of some of the larger function rooms in the Lacey house for business conventions.'

There was a little buzz of comment and he paused.

'Kiloran and her grandfather have also agreed to sell the Augustus John, which you may be aware is solely their property. The profit raised will be channelled directly back into the business.' He looked around, gauging their reaction. 'I cannot see that anyone here today could have any objections to either of those two strategies, particularly as Kiloran and her grandfather have agreed to them, and they are the people who will be hardest hit by either.'

Aunt Jacqueline gave a giggle. 'Heavens! You'll be running an up-market guest house! What does your mother have to say about *that*?'

'She understands that there's no alternative,' answered Kiloran, in a low voice. She had rung her mother late last night to tell her.

'But hasn't she offered her rich husband to bail you out?' asked Jacqueline mischievously.

Adam's mouth curved, glad to be reminded of reality rather than hormone-driven fantasy. Was that the philosophy among the Lacey women, then? Men as open cheque-books? Flutter your eyelashes and they'd always help you out in a fix. Though, if that were the case—then why hadn't Kiloran tried it? He didn't imagine that she would have *any* trouble netting a rich sugar-daddy.

Kiloran saw his brief look of distaste and winced. 'That wasn't an option,' she said quietly. 'I'll be opening the function rooms for business conventions—just as stately homes do these days.'

'I think it's a wonderful idea,' breathed Julia, and, when Adam turned to look at her, her mouth fell slightly open, gleaming and parted provocatively. 'I never liked that old drawing anyway—*much* too dark!'

Kiloran looked down at the polished table, despairing at her cousin's reaction. Old drawing, indeed! She loved that etching—both subtle and yet highly erotic. It showed a woman drying herself after a bath; the economical lines used by the artist managed to perfectly convey the gleaming, wet flesh.

It had hung in that room for as long as *she* could remember, and it had hung there during her mother's childhood, and her grandfather's—and before even that. Was it so wrong to want to safeguard the past?

She glanced up to find Adam watching her, surprising a disconcerting flash of understanding in the grey eyes.

'I don't think any of us underestimate the sacrifice

in parting with something so deeply cherished,' he said quietly. 'Now, shall we take a vote on it?'

The rest was a mere formality. The vote was carried and passed and the meeting broke up to adjourn for the drinks which stood waiting on the side.

It all seemed a bit of an anticlimax and Kiloran wanted to leave, and to leave as quickly as possible, but she knew that would have been rude. The shareholders would be expecting their pound of flesh, and that included talking to her. She kept her chatter bright and enthusiastic, trying not to focus on Adam, but that would have been like trying not to notice a meteor which had come crashing through the ceiling.

You couldn't miss him, or his low, murmured laugh. And neither did she miss the fact that Julia was commandeering his attention, or that he was letting her, though she guessed she shouldn't be surprised. Julia would turn most men's heads with more than just her looks—she had the kind of kittenish compliance which most men found irresistible.

She belonged to the school which thought that men should be flattered and cajoled and pampered. An old-fashioned view that men were always right—their jokes listened to attentively and laughed at whether they were funny or not. Julia had been engaged three times before changing her mind at the last minute, leaving broken-hearted swains in her wake, so the submissive attitude clearly worked.

And Adam obviously thought so, too—judging from the way he was responding. Unwillingly, Kiloran looked at them. His dark head was bent as Julia raised herself up on tiptoe to whisper into his ear and he laughed at something she said.

Kiloran put her glass down. She was damned if she was going to stand and watch while those two heads grew ever closer, while Julia moved in for the kill, with Adam the willing victim.

Taking a deep breath, she walked towards them and her cousin shot her a 'lucky-me' look.

'Adam, I'm going now.'

Adam thought how pale she looked and wondered if this meeting had been a trial. Perhaps she considered it a complete waste of her time—to have travelled up to London just to have his plan rubber-stamped—but common courtesy had insisted that she be there. And it had all been resolved very smoothly, hadn't it? So why was her face so tense? Her green eyes looked almost haunted and there were tiny goose bumps on her bare arms.

He found himself transfixed by the golden cross attached to a fine gold chain which hung around her neck and which dipped tantalisingly towards the hollow created by her breasts. He hadn't been able to get her out of his mind, and now he found he didn't want to let her out of his sight.

And when he spoke, his voice sounded husky. 'Kiloran, you can't possibly leave yet. Stay for another drink.'

It was tempting, particularly if she drank with him, but then she noticed that both he and Julia were drinking champagne—and what had she got to celebrate?

'No. Honestly. Thanks. I must get back—I've got a lot to do.'

'Yes.' There was something so ethereal about her at that moment, she looked as if a puff of wind might blow her away. He remembered how the sunlight had illuminated her blonde hair like a halo in the garden, how he had told her things which might have been best left unsaid. A confession which had troubled him, but more because of the fact that he had made it—and to whom—than because of its content. He held his hand out. 'Goodbye, then, Kiloran.'

She shook his hand, revelling in that one, brief moment of contact and wondering, if circumstances had been different, whether she might have got to know him on an altogether different level. 'Goodbye, Adam. And thank you.'

She gave Julia a kiss on either cheek, said goodbye to her aunt Jacqueline and ran for the tube, but as the train raced through the dark tunnels she couldn't get him out of her head. Stop building him up into some kind of romantic fantasy, she told herself. What would be the point? Just forget him.

For the next few weeks she did her best to do just that.

The first thing she did was to contact an auctioneer with a view to selling the etching by auction, and the delightful if rather foppish man who came to see it grew very excited.

'Oh, this is very special,' he breathed. 'Very special indeed. We shan't have any problem finding a buyer for *this*.' He looked at her. 'Shame to have to sell it?'

Kiloran nodded. 'It *is* sad,' she agreed. 'But it's not the end of the world.' She gave him a bright, determined smile. It was more than just wanting to put things right—she was going to show Adam Black that it *could* be done—and that she could do it.

Next she rang up the Council to find out what she needed to do about letting out rooms. There was lots to discuss—planning permission, health and safety, building regulations. When all the paperwork had been done, a very officious woman came to the house to tell her that there would have to be slight modifications made to the vast Lacey kitchen and that the bathroom facilities would have to be extended, all of which could be quickly accomplished.

She thawed a little when Kiloran gave her tea and lemon cake. 'You might as well start advertising in the business journals straight away,' she suggested as her large teeth bit into a piece of lemon icing. 'No time like the present!'

Photographs were taken of the house and gardens and a full-page spread was placed in *Investment Today!*

'Don't scrimp on advertising,' warned the magazine. 'It's a false economy. Targeting the right client is essential.'

Building work began and Kiloran persuaded her grandfather to make a trip to see her mother in Australia. He had been meaning to do so for a while, and having scaffolding and debris around the place finally goaded him into action.

'I can't keep putting it off,' he said to Kiloran rather wistfully.

She understood what he was saying. He was an old man. He could not keep putting things off. You had to live for the moment, she thought as she drove him and his nurse to Heathrow, while the memory of Adam's smile swam into her mind to haunt her.

The police were no closer to finding Eddie Peterhouse, but suddenly that no longer seemed to matter. Lacey's was safe, the staff had lost their edge of worry. Adam had shown her a way out, and she was taking it.

She thought about him, of course—even though she had vowed not to. Someone that dynamic wasn't easily forgettable. And even though she fell into bed exhausted at the end of every day, she dreamt about him, too—and dreams she had no control over, unlike her thoughts. The unconscious mind was so powerful, and so, too, were the sensual, erotic dreams which made her sleep fitful, and left her waking shaken.

The first tang of autumn was in the air when an envelope fell through the letter box. It was an invitation to Julia's birthday party and Kiloran put it on the mantelpiece and forgot all about it, until she got a phone call from Julia herself.

'Well?' she demanded. 'Are you coming?'

'Oh, heck,' groaned Kiloran. 'I've been so busy, I forgot all about it. When is it?'

'Saturday.'

'Saturday?' Kiloran frowned again. '*This* Saturday?'

'That's what it said on the invitation!'

Kiloran sat on the edge of the desk. She had been working almost non-stop since Adam had left. Maybe a party was just what she needed.

'Yes, I'd love to come, Jules.'

'By the way…' there was a pause '…I've invited Adam.'

Kiloran's heart raced. 'Oh?' she said, hoping that her tone conveyed just the right amount of noncommittal interest, but inside her stomach was sinking. All the signs had been there—was Julia going out with Adam?

'Yes.' There was a sigh. 'Wish I hadn't bothered really, but there's nothing I can do about it now.'

'Oh,' said Kiloran again.

Another sigh. 'I made a bit of a play for him and, for the first time in my life, found a man who wasn't willing to take the bait—not just unwilling, but not *interested*, either! Did my ego the world of good, I can tell you,' Julia added wryly.

For some inexplicable reason, the answer to her next question was terribly important. 'And you're heartbroken, right?'

'Wrong!' Julia laughed. 'For about a minute maybe! Then I found myself a suitable replacement. Well, he's tall and he's rich and he's handsome! He's not Adam Black but maybe that's a good thing. I like a man you can tame and he doesn't strike me as a tameable man—not by any stretch of the imagination. You like him, don't you, Kiloran?' she added casually.

'My views on Adam Black correspond pretty much to yours,' said Kiloran slowly.

'So we'll definitely see you on Saturday?'

'Yeah. Looking forward to it.' Kiloran replaced the receiver with a heavy feeling in her heart. She didn't want to face him; she didn't—but having said she would go, she could hardly back out now, could she? What if Julia told him that she had agreed to go and then changed her mind when she had heard that *he* was going? Why give him that pleasure?

What the hell? She *would* go! And I can slip away early, she decided. No one will notice.

She dressed for the party with inordinate care, using clothes as an armoury.

She wore scarlet. Deliberately. Bright and bold and dramatic. The colour of blood and of life and against it her blonde hair contrasted as pale as the waning moon.

The dress was not especially revealing, but it clung like a second skin, moulding itself to her hips and the lush swell of her breasts, the skirt swirling a little when she walked in a pair of deliciously high-heeled black shoes. She piled her hair up on her head and secured it with glittery scarlet pins, so that tendrils of it tumbled and twisted around her face. With her green eyes and her scarlet lips she thought that she looked more like a doll than a living, breathing woman, but she didn't care.

She took the car. At least that way she would be independent. No need to stay the night in town, or to be reliant on a train which might or might not run on time.

But once she hit London, the traffic was absolutely atrocious. She sat for what seemed like an eternity in a jam and, by the time she drew up close to Julia's house, was nearly two hours late and wished she had the nerve to turn around and go straight back again.

Oh, for heaven's sake, she told herself crossly. Since when did you decide to start acting like a love-lorn schoolgirl? He probably wouldn't even *be* there now. And it wasn't even as though she had anything concrete on which to pin her fantasies, was it? Apart from a sexual attraction which only a fool would have denied—this was the way which every woman on the planet probably felt towards him. He had done absolutely nothing to encourage her.

With a heavy heart, she got out of her car outside the Chelsea town house to hear music spilling out, and she had to ring twice before anyone heard her.

A girl she had never seen before answered the door, clutching a tumbler of lurid-coloured cocktail. 'Hi!' she said brightly, and peered at her rather drunkenly. 'Who're you?'

'I'm Kiloran—Julia's cousin.'

'She's inside somewhere,' said the girl vaguely. 'Come on in.'

Inside, the music was throbbing and there were people everywhere. Kiloran looked around for Julia, but couldn't see her. In fact, she couldn't see a single soul she knew and that only increased her feeling of isolation.

She headed for the kitchen, where she managed to fight her way through the scrum to find herself a glass of wine, and then made her way back towards the party.

The first reception room was crammed to bursting, with couples glued together under the guise of dancing.

The second was still crowded, but there was at least room to stand and, in an effort to find Julia, Kiloran began to push her way forward, when she froze.

Because he was there.

Difficult to see, true, because he was surrounded by a nucleus of glamorous women who seemed to be straining towards him, drawn like iron filings to a magnet.

But his presence was as unmistakable as it was remarkable. That tall, wide-shouldered yet lean body. The jet-dark hair and the glittering stormy eyes. And before they could be trained in her direction Kiloran fled—making her way back through the kitchen and out into the garden, like someone seeking sanctuary.

The air was surprisingly clean and pure and scented, with only the faint drone of traffic reminding her that she was in the city. Kiloran took a sip of her drink, but the wine almost made her choke when she sensed, rather than heard, someone behind her and she spun round to see the tall, dark figure watching her, unmoving, the grey eyes unreadable, and she stood, rooted to the spot, as if she were part of the garden itself.

He had seen her, of course. Through the smoke and

the cloying perfume and the dazzle of the party outfits he had noticed her pale blonde hair and scarlet dress immediately.

And a small smile had lifted the corners of his hard mouth as he had observed her hurried departure from the room. Had she known, or expected—that he would follow her?

Well, he had.

'Hello, Kiloran,' he said softly.

Kiloran swallowed. 'H-hi.'

He felt his heart accelerate as he moved towards her. The colour of the dress she wore was as hot as a flame and yet she still carried with her that cool and untouchable air about her, which was ironic really, considering that she looked as though she had been born just for a man's touch. His touch.

His mouth tightened as he drank in the lush curves, the whisper of silk against the endless legs—pale and slim—made longer still by the outrageously high heels she was wearing.

He had tried not to think about her, and yet had done nothing *but* think about her. Yet she seemed to represent some inexplicable danger and he couldn't work out why. Was it because circumstances had made him tell her something of his past? Allowed her access to a side of himself he usually kept concealed from the world?

But as the days had gone on the danger had seemed to become something to be faced rather than to be avoidable. He hadn't realised how much he had been waiting for this moment until now.

Kiloran's heart thudded at the expression she read in his eyes—predatory, sensual, full of promise.

'You're looking very…spectacular,' he said carefully.

So was he. Oh, so was he! 'It *is* a party,' she said equally carefully. This close she could see the faint shadow around his jaw, the dark crisp sprinkling of hair revealed by the couple of buttons of his white silk shirt which he had undone.

He put his glass down on the table. 'I hear things are going very well for you.'

She gave him a cool smile. 'I like to think so. We've sold the etching.'

'So I gather. Well done. It must have been a wrench.'

She gave him a quick glance, sensing sarcasm, but the expression on his face made him look as though he had meant it.

Kiloran thought how different he seemed tonight. In the office she had caught only glimpses of his devastating sensual nature, but tonight that man was revealed in all his unmistakable glory.

'Miss me?' he mocked.

She met the challenge in his eyes. 'What do you think?'

'I think that maybe you do.'

'You really are unbelievable, Adam,' she murmured.

'So I've been told.'

'That wasn't what I meant and you know it!'

Her eyes were lit with green fire and her mouth was

a soft, scarlet invitation. How he had hungered for her, and now his appetite was growing by the minute.

'It wasn't such a terrible assumption to make, was it, Kiloran? It's just that I missed you and thought that perhaps the feeling might be mutual.'

Her heart skipped a beat. 'You—*missed* me?'

'Mmm.' He wanted to reach his hand out and free her hair, clip by scarlet clip. 'I wasn't expecting to, but I did.'

'Is that supposed to be a compliment?'

His grey eyes shone as he shook his dark, ruffled head. 'Only if you take it as one. It's the truth—nothing more, nothing less.'

There was something ominous about that. Nothing more, nothing less. As if he was setting out some guidelines. Instinct told her to get away from him while she still had the ability to do so, but some unfathomable emotion tempted her to stay. 'Well, now I'm here.'

'Yes.' His eyes drifted over her and when he spoke the one word was delivered so softly that she could barely hear it.

'Look.'

She followed the direction of his gaze as he positioned his finger a hair's breadth away from the tiny goose bumps at the top of her arm and traced an imaginary line right down to her wrist. He wasn't even touching her and yet inside she felt as if she were turning to jelly. She stared at him.

'See?' he whispered. 'The evening is warm and yet you're cold and trembling. And your eyes are flashing a complex message at me. On the one hand you look as if you would like me as far away from you as possible, while, on the other, as if there was nowhere else you'd rather be. So which is it to be, Kiloran?'

'The former,' she breathed.

'No,' he contradicted.

'Oh, yes. I nearly pulled out when I heard you were coming,' she told him.

For some reason, this stirred him even more. 'Well, I did the opposite. I came because I knew you would be here. Because I wanted to see you again and thought you might look very beautiful. And you do. Very.'

Kiloran despised the frantic beat of her heart which raced in response to the honeyed caress of his voice. 'You could have rung me up any time, if you'd wanted to see me.'

'But I prefer the unexpected,' he said softly. 'I wanted to see the look on your face when you saw me, and I wasn't disappointed.'

Oh, Lord—did that mean she had completely given herself away?

His eyes were drifting over her now—unashamed predator. He still carried with him the indefinable air of control, but tonight the mask had slipped slightly.

'Stop it.'

'But why,' he questioned softly, taking the glass from her unprotesting fingers and placing it on the table next to his, 'when you don't want me to stop it?'

'Yes, I do,' she whispered, but he must have read the lie in her eyes and on her lips.

'I don't think so. It's been tough at work—but we're no longer at work. I've left and we're free to do what the hell we want. We've been fighting it and I don't want to fight it any more. I know what you want, honey.'

'Stop it,' she whispered again, but he took no notice, just gave a low laugh as he caught her by the waist, drawing her behind the scented seclusion of the thick, scrambling honeysuckle and into his arms.

'Say it once more—with feeling,' he whispered.

Say it? She could scarcely breathe, her senses were so full of him and the heady perfume of the flowers. He pulled her closer and bent his head to look down into her face, his dark features leaning over her with a look of desire which she had dreamt of. But the reality far outstripped the dream. Dreams were cold, comfortless illusions while reality pulsed with life and promise.

But wasn't desire on its own wrong? Shouldn't there be something more than that? 'Don't—' The protest was blotted out by his kiss, her word drowned by that first sweet, melting contact, and she said his name in a kind of broken assent. 'Adam.'

'I know.' His words were a shuddering sigh as he cupped her face between the palms of his hands and plundered more deeply, coaxing her mouth open with the tip of his tongue until she could bear it no more and her lips finally parted to let him dip inside, into a sweet moistness that made him groan.

Kiloran felt as if she had strayed unawares into an unknown country where sensation ruled supreme.

Every nerve-ending was screaming in sensory alert, her body flowering into instant life beneath the urgent possession of his mouth. Her blood growing thick and heated. Her heart pounding, threatening to leap out of her chest.

She gave herself up to it—it simply wasn't within her power not to as her eyelids fluttered to a close. Somehow her hands had drifted up to grip the broad, hard shoulders, feeling the sinew beneath the thin silk of the shirt he wore.

One hand had moved from her face to cup her buttock, moving her body closer still, so that they were moulded unbearably close together, her skin on fire where it touched his, her mouth making an involuntary moan as she felt the stark, hard power of him where the cradle of his masculinity pressed unashamedly against her.

The kiss went on and on until Adam drew his mouth away, staring down into the huge, haunted green eyes, at the soft, dark blossom of her lips.

'Maybe we'd better stop this,' he managed unsteadily.

Her breathing was ragged as she gazed up at him in befuddlement, just wanting him to carry on kissing her.

'Come home with me, Kiloran,' he urged softly.

It took a moment or two for it to register exactly what it was he was saying and when she did it was powerful enough to annihilate the terrible longing. Just like that! The cold, hard, commitment-phobe Adam Black thought that one kiss would have her in his bed within minutes! And if she had been drowning under his kiss, then now was the time to come up for air. And fast.

She smoothed her ruffled hair back. 'Isn't it mandatory to at least buy a woman dinner first?' she questioned drily.

His eyes glittered. The untouchable look was back, and somehow that turned him on even more. 'You're hungry?'

'You really do have the most colossal nerve, don't you, Adam?' she demanded icily.

'No man has ever kissed you at a party, is that it?'

Not like that, they hadn't, no. 'That's not the point!' she snapped. 'Most women require a little more wooing than one kiss followed by the careless suggestion they might like to share your bed!'

'You want me, Kiloran,' he said unsteadily. 'Deny that and I'll call you a liar!'

She wasn't stupid enough to deny what was as plain as the faint outline of the moon which was beginning to appear in the still-blue sky. 'I might want a diamond necklace—but that doesn't mean I'm automatically going to rush out and rob the first jeweller's I see!' He began to laugh as she pushed one of the dangling tendrils away from her cheek and began to turn away, afraid that her face would reveal more than he knew. More than even she knew, because, surely to goodness, a single kiss shouldn't make her feel like this— as if she had never known what it was to really *feel* before? 'Goodbye, Adam.'

'And where are you going?'

'Home. Back to Lacey's.' Back to where she was safe—safe from a man with nothing to offer but his exquisite body. She turned back then, surer of herself. 'And please don't try following me!'

He didn't point out that her eyes belied her words. No woman wanted to be made aware of her own weaknesses.

'No, I won't follow you,' he murmured softly. 'Not tonight. I've done enough deals in my life to know that you should only act when the moment is right, and that moment isn't now. I'm good at waiting—I always have been. And I'll only come when you're ready for me, Kiloran.'

CHAPTER EIGHT

WITH Adam's mocking words ringing in her ears, Kiloran drove back to the house in a highly charged state of arousal and indignation.

So he would come back when she was ready, would he? As if she were some package just waiting for him to open her! As if he could walk into her life and find her waiting there with open arms.

But the memory of his kiss burned on her lips as if he had branded her. As if he had made her his with just that one stamp of possession.

She fought it all the way home, telling herself that she was completely in control. He had coaxed her body into glorious and responsive life, but that didn't mean that she was going to leap into bed with him. In fact, when he came—*if* he came—she would just show him the door.

But he didn't come.

And somehow, instead of dampening the fire he had ignited, his failure to show only fanned the flames and it was hard to think of anything but him, even though she tried.

She threw herself into her work as more and more was accomplished on the conversion of the house. The newly revamped kitchen looked almost unrecognisable and the reception rooms gleamed with new paint.

And although she was spending long hours in the office, Kiloran forced herself to accept every invitation which came her way. There were cocktail parties and dinner parties and balls, and when she wasn't socialising she rode her horse until her muscles ached and exhaustion claimed her and the memory of him grew fainter.

Until one evening, nearly six weeks later, when she returned from the stables to find him waiting for her, and her heart missed a beat for it was like every fantasy come true.

A silver sports car was parked directly in front of the house, and a dark figure dressed completely in black leaned against it. Her throat dried as she met that laconic, glittering gaze and she felt like someone who had spent days in the desert as she drank in the hard, cold features and the luscious, carved mouth.

He had come.

She walked towards him, her heart pounding, wondering if her excitement showed, feeling her palms grow damp and clammy as she gave him what she hoped was a noncommittal smile.

'Adam,' she said. 'This is a surprise.'

'I said I would come.' He had kept her waiting until he himself could wait no longer. A smile glimmered its way to the corners of his mouth. She was wearing riding clothes! Excitement began to fizz its way through his veins as he took in the tight jodhpurs, the long, leather boots and the silk shirt, clinging damply to her breasts. 'And here I am.'

'So I...see.' The dark jeans emphasised the long,

muscular legs and the fine cashmere sweater matched his dark, ruffled hair. He was so damned sure of himself. And his arrogance and conceit filled her with a new strength.

She raised her eyebrows questioningly. 'Why?'

'I thought you might like to have dinner with me.'

'Dinner as a precursor to sex, is that what you mean?'

He feigned outraged surprise. 'Kiloran,' he murmured. 'You shock me.'

'Then you're easily shocked,' she retorted. 'Don't tell me you want to have dinner because you want to get to know me better as a person.'

'Yes,' he said unexpectedly. 'I do. Now who's looking shocked? What's the matter, Kiloran—do you think I'm so crass that I just want to take you to bed and that's it?'

'That's what you suggested the other night.'

'I was a little carried away by the heat of the moment.'

'And if I'd said yes? One night of bliss and that would have been that?'

'I'm flattered you anticipate bliss,' he purred, before giving his dark head a shake of exasperation. 'But, no, I'm not into one-night stands.'

'But you're not into commitment either.' Now why on earth had she said *that*?

'Not if you're talking wedding bells and happy ever after,' he agreed.

'Stop twisting it round,' she protested. 'I'm not proposing marriage!'

He laughed. 'I'm very relieved to hear it.' His eyes drifted across her face, lingering longest on her lips, wanting to kiss them again. 'So how about dinner, Kiloran?'

She thought about what it would entail. The drive to the nearest pub or restaurant. The fussing around with drinks and menus. A waitress disturbing their conversation. Onlookers when she wanted to be alone with him. 'I'm not hungry,' she said truthfully.

There was a heartbeat of a pause. 'No. Neither am I.'

Kiloran's tongue flicked out to slick at her parched lips. There was something so *blatant* about the way he was looking at her. No other man could have got away with such unashamed hunger. 'You know…' she swallowed '…you wouldn't win any prizes for subtlety.'

'I'm not looking to.' His eyes narrowed. 'And subtlety isn't my style, Kiloran. I prefer honesty. I see what I want and I go all out to get it. And I want you.'

She gave a shaky laugh. Men didn't come out and say things like that—they might think it, but they didn't *say* it! 'Just like that? Is this the line you spin to every woman?'

'I don't usually have to.' Most women would have gone straight back to bed with him the night of the party.

'They make it easy for you?'

'Or easy for themselves?'

'Arrogance!' But she laughed in spite of herself.

'Just truth.'

He leaned against the car and the jut of his hips was like an open invitation. Kiloran looked him straight in the eye. 'I'm not interested in being one of a long line of willing victims.'

He thought that *victim* was an unusual choice of word. 'I'm not as indiscriminate as you seem to imply, Kiloran,' he said softly.

'No? So when did you last have a lover?'

He frowned with memory, and the wry knowledge that, having admitted honesty, he could not now refuse to answer her question. 'Back in the States—a little under a year ago.' He met her eyes. 'Hardly evidence of a man who's engaged on a mission to seduce every woman in sight—no matter what my reputation. Satisfied, Kiloran?'

It was an ironic and poor choice of word. Satisfied was the last word she would use to describe herself, not when he was looking at her with those smoky grey eyes, his thumb hooked lazily into the belt of his trousers. Promising everything, promising nothing.

'This isn't what I'm used to,' she admitted. It felt too sophisticated, too calculating. Too lacking in emotion. For him, certainly. But that didn't stop her wanting it. The only question was, did she dare run the risk of getting hurt?

He nodded. 'You want me to send flowers, is that it?'

'I have all the flowers I need, Adam.'

'So are you going to play games with me, honey? Tease me a little longer? Play the dance of convention? Or are you going to come over here and put us both out of our misery?'

He ran his eyes over her with a proprietorial air which made her heart begin to race erratically. She wanted to run straight into his arms, but an instinct for self-preservation stopped her. 'Just what are you offering me, Adam?' she asked quietly. 'Honestly?'

'Honestly?' Her directness was almost refreshing—if it wasn't such a bloody challenge! 'A relationship—if that's what you want, and I think you do. No strings. No demands. No ties. No questions.'

'Fidelity?'

His eyes narrowed. 'Always.'

'And if I hadn't turned up to Julia's party, what then? Would someone else have done?' But deep down she knew the answer to this. And it was not ego but a sure sense of her own self-worth that made her realise that he was not just looking for a willing body. He could have had scores of those.

'No, Kiloran, no one else would have done. It would have been another time, but I would have still ended up having exactly this conversation with you.'

'I should kick you out right here and now,' she whispered.

'But you aren't going to. Are you?'

No, she wasn't. But neither was she going to fall like a ripe plum from a tree straight into his arms. Even though the taut, hungry set of his body told her that this was what he expected. 'Would you like to come inside?' She gave him her politest smile. 'And have some tea after your long drive?'

She was putting him in his place, and for a moment he enjoyed the unfamiliar sensation of subordination. 'Served by one of your army of staff?' he questioned drily as he fell into step beside her.

She pushed open the back door. 'Hardly an army, Adam. Though, as it happens, I've been cooking for myself since Grandfather went to Australia.'

'Have you now? I'm impressed.' But she had bent over to pull off one of her riding boots and he thought that he might explode when he saw the jodhpurs tighten over the curve of her bottom. It seemed like an eternity before both boots were kicked off in a muddy heap and they tramped through into the kitchen.

'Indian?' she asked, pulling the elastic band confining her damp hair and shaking it free. 'Or China?'

The movement of her breasts as her hair came down entranced him and he knew that tea would choke him. She turned to face him and he met a look of startled recognition in her eyes, a hunger which matched and fed his own.

'You don't want tea,' he said huskily and pulled her into his arms. 'Any more than you want dinner. This is what you want, isn't it, honey?'

Of course it was—but still some small voice of sanity tried to reason with her. Pull away, she told herself. Even though he's strong, he won't stop you. Even though he's aroused, he will let you go. But she didn't pull away. 'Adam,' she said threadily.

'Kiloran,' he mocked, but his voice was thick with need as he drove his mouth down on hers with a kiss which ignited all the pent-up longing which had been eating away inside him. 'Kiloran,' he breathed against her mouth. 'I can't wait any more.'

For so strong and so powerful a man, it was an unexpected note of surrender, and surrender where it was least expected had a potent power of its own. It sealed what the kiss had started, and the slow blaze erupted into flames, setting her on fire where their bodies touched.

She caught his shoulders, her fingers sliding luxuriously against the sensual black cashmere, making a mixed moan of protest and delight as he began to unbutton the thin silk shirt which clung damply to her breasts, peeling it away so that her breasts were revealed, the golden-white flesh spilling over creamy lace.

'Oh, my,' he murmured as he gazed down at them, bending his head to flick a lazy tongue over where a raspberry-dark nipple protruded, hearing her tiny little gasp of pleasure as he felt it peak against his tongue.

Her hands burrowed up beneath the cashmere, feeling skin as silkily sensuous as the sweater itself, the muscles hard and firm beneath the oiled flesh. She could feel the slick rush of heat and her heart was racing out of control as his mouth whispered a slow, erotic trail of delight over her breasts. 'Adam,' she managed.

'Are we alone?' His breath felt warm against her skin.

It was what they called the sixty-four-thousand-dollar question. She nodded. 'Completely,' she whispered.

He lifted his head to stare down at her. The cool, untouchable Kiloran Lacey was barely recognisable. Her eyes were huge, so glitteringly black that the emerald rims were barely visible. Two flares of rose-pink defined the high, aristocratic cheekbones and her mouth was like a crushed rose. He ran his finger along the curve of her jaw and felt her tremble in instant response and knew that he could have her here. Now. On this great big wide oak table which looked as if it had been here since the beginning of time.

But he needed something to calm him, something which would not have him acting as if he had never made love to a woman before, which was exactly how he felt.

With a swift, decisive movement he bent and scooped her up into his arms and her head fell back.

'What's this?' she whispered.

'You look like some old-fashioned stable wench,' he managed unsteadily. 'So I might as well play my part, too. Shall I carry you upstairs to have my wicked way with you?'

'W-wicked?'

'Very wicked. Does that suit you, Kiloran?'

Oh—yes! At that moment he was the master and she the slave and she had never felt more deliciously weak. His curved smile of expectation was tinged with danger, and the glitter of his eyes indicated that he, too, was on a knife-edge of control.

In a silence broken only by the sound of their

breathing, he carried her upstairs. The irony of the fact that he was playing the dominant role and she the subservient one didn't escape her—but the fantasy was impossible to resist. At that moment he *did* dominate—by the sheer force of his personality and his formidable sexuality, and Kiloran Lacey rejoiced in the feeling that a man could make her feel like this.

He was staring down into her hot face, at the hectic glitter of her eyes. 'Where?' he shot out.

'In—there.' She pointed a shaky finger at the second door of the west wing and he pushed it open with his knee, depositing her in the centre of the four-poster, and then looked down at her, a fierce and intense look of longing darkening his features.

'Am I your master?' he questioned silkily.

The fact that he had clicked right into her own fantasy made her want him even more. 'Yes,' she whispered, from between parched lips.

'Then take my sweater off,' he instructed.

But she felt so weak that she couldn't have moved from the spot, drowning in sweet anticipation. 'No.'

He smiled. 'So you're going to defy me, are you, Kiloran? You're going to force me to strip for you?'

The roles were now reversed and, wordlessly, she nodded, watching with unbearable excitement as he peeled the sweater off and tossed it aside, then began to unbuckle the belt of his black jeans, his eyes not leaving her face.

He kicked his shoes off, then unzipped the trousers slowly, provocatively, wincing very slightly as they rasped down over the undisguisable evidence of how aroused he was, and despite her hunger, her excitement, colour flared in Kiloran's cheeks and he smiled.

'Am I making you feel shy?' he purred.

'A little.'

He slid the jeans down over the hard, muscular shafts of his thighs, kicking them off impatiently, until he was wearing absolutely nothing but a pair of boxer shorts, their silken sheen emphasising the hard outline of his erection.

With a sinful smile he slid them off and Kiloran gave an involuntary gasp.

Totally unselfconscious in his nakedness, he came to lie on the bed beside her, but he didn't touch her and she turned to him, a little pout of frustration crumpling her lips.

His eyes were slitted, the thick, dark lashes hiding all but a steely gleam. 'Your turn now.'

'But I want *you* to undress me—'

He shook his head. 'Next time,' he promised.

'No. This time.'

He leaned over her, sensing the battle and wondering whose nerve would break first, and recognising from the implacable light of determination in her eyes that it would be him. For a man used to winning, it excited him beyond reason and his mouth curved almost cruelly.

'So that's the way you want it, is it?' he murmured.

His touch seemed to burn sweet, pure fire on her skin as he began to remove her clothes with enchanting yet frustrating precision. The damp shirt was discarded and then he unclipped her bra, tossing the flimsy piece of lace aside, his fingertips lingering on each breast, ignoring her sighing little objection when they did no more but whisper and tease.

He eased the jodhpurs down over her pale, milky thighs and then skimmed the lacy little thong the same way. And only then did he lean over her, blotting out the light which streamed in through the windows, promising so much with the lean, hard contours of his body, yet his tense face yielding no emotion as he stared down at her.

'You are every man's fantasy come to living, breathing life,' he said unsteadily.

But the beautiful mouth was unsmiling as he bent his lips to her breast.

A pierce of longing so sharp that it came close to pain shot through her, her head falling helplessly back against the pillow, her eyes closed as his fingertips began to weave their magic on her body.

'Adam,' she choked, and wondered if she sounded as vulnerable as she felt at that moment.

'Tell me,' he urged, lifting his head. 'Or show me.'

Blindly, she reached her arms up to him, pulling him down, wanting his kiss, and when it came it was everything a kiss should be—seeking, urgent, satisfying and yet curiously unsatisfying, leaving her wanting more. And more still. Giving her a fleeting premonition that whatever Adam Black gave her it would never be enough.

His hand moved over the slight swell of her belly and then down to the juncture of her thighs, finding the moist, heated centre of her, hearing her helpless little cry.

She was like malleable clay beneath his expert touch, but he was doing all the giving and suddenly the game of power and control seemed unimportant. She reached out and took him in her hand, enjoying his automatic little jerk of pleasure as she began to move her palm softly over his silken hardness.

'What are you trying to do?' he gasped. 'Kill me?'

If 'orgasm' was translated from the French as 'a little death' then, yes, she would like to give him the most slow, pleasurable one imaginable, but he shook his head, his face tight with tension.

'Not now.' He wanted to join with her, to feel the most basic communion of all—the melding of flesh and of senses.

He pushed into her before she was expecting it and her eyes flew open, a delicious slow heat beginning to spread over her.

'Adam—'

'What?' he whispered back and began to move slowly, his eyes locking hers, a soft smile making him look almost vulnerable.

She had forgotten this intimacy—it had been a long time—but she had never been roused to this kind of pitch before, either, not even within the context of a long-term relationship. She had said 'I love you' to a man before at just this moment, but now she realised that those could be words said as convention, not because you felt as though you would die if you didn't say them.

She wanted to say them now, to Adam, and she had to bite them back, telling herself that she couldn't possibly love him. She didn't know him well enough to love him—it was just great sex, that was all.

'Adam!'

'Mmm?'

Did he sense that already she was so close to the edge? Did her body relay that to him and he respond with long, hard strokes which felt as though they were piercing her heart itself?

'Adam, it's—'

It was too late, for her and for him. He felt the great, swamping rush of pleasure before his world exploded, to the sensation of her sweet, pulsing flesh and her choked little cry, and the astonishing sound of him saying her name, over and over and over again.

Kiloran watched the man who slept beside her. The rumpled duvet lay skimming his narrow hips, leaving his torso naked, and his chest rose and fell with the deep, rhythmic breaths of a truly relaxed sleep.

She stared at his face. The dark lashes formed two perfect arcs which rested like feathers on the sculpted features and his lips were very slightly parted, almost begging to be kissed.

But she didn't lean across and kiss them. After what they had just shared that seemed like an intimacy too far. A wave of dark hair curled over his forehead and she wanted to wind it round her finger.

But she didn't do that, either.

She knew the big things about him—that he was

intelligent and dynamic and powerful and that he was an achiever. That he drove a fancy silver car and lived in London and had experienced loss and betrayal in his youth, which probably accounted for why he had never settled down.

The big things, yes, but not the little things. Like whether he hated being woken from sleep, or whether he drank tea in bed in the mornings. Or whether…

Grey eyes flickered lazily open and he gave a slow smile, running a reflective finger along the curved outline of her naked body. It was a moment before he spoke and, when he did, his voice sounded reflective. 'That was pretty amazing, Kiloran.'

Suddenly, stupidly, she felt shy—as if she were being given marks out of ten for performance.

The finger moved to tilt her chin. 'Wasn't it?' he prompted.

'You know it was.'

'But you're regretting it?'

She felt her body stiffen. 'Why should I?'

'Because you look a little…wary…I guess.'

That was because she was. She had taken as a lover a man who she could see as being nothing more than that. A passionate man with coolly assessing eyes which promised everything and yet promised nothing. Was she setting herself up for automatic heartbreak? Shouldn't she have given it more thought than she had done, rather than letting him kiss away any lingering doubts? But passion was a strange and capricious emotion. Normal rules did not apply. And, besides, it was too late now.

'Do I?' she said lightly.

'You know you do—now wipe that frown away and come here.'

He caught hold of her and brought her face down to kiss him, so that her hair dangled and tickled at his chest and Kiloran remembered that she had come straight from the stables. 'I must look a fright,' she groaned, jerking her head back.

'You look gorgeous.'

'Liar!'

'But I never lie,' he reminded her softly.

'Do I smell of horses?'

He rubbed his nose against her neck and breathed in. 'Mmm. A little.'

'Why didn't you tell me?'

'It turned me on, if you must know.'

'I could have taken a bath,' she said shakily, because something in the way he was looking at her was making her feel so *wanton*.

'There wasn't time.' His eyes grew smoky as they captured hers. 'We could take one now, if you like.'

She felt him grow hard against her and slid her arm around his waist. 'Okay,' she said breathlessly.

'And then you can show me your newly acquired cooking skills. And then we can make love again.' Idly, he began to stroke at a rosy nipple and felt it spring into instant life. 'And then we can co-ordinate our diaries.'

Kiloran's hand stopped stroking the satin skin in the small of his back. 'Diaries?' she asked stupidly.

'I want to know when I'm going to see you again.'

CHAPTER NINE

CO-ORDINATING their diaries.

It wasn't the most romantic way to begin a relationship, though Kiloran supposed that it was the prac-
tical way, particularly in view of the fact that Adam
had recently started a new job—doing what he had
been brought in to do at Lacey's, only on a much
larger scale.

'I'm going to be pretty tied up next week,' he had
said as he'd bent his head to kiss her goodbye. 'But
I'll ring you.'

And immediately she was catapulted into that unwilling state of waiting for the phone to ring.

He didn't ring until Wednesday, which she supposed was about right for the kind of relationship they
were obviously going to have and the kind of man he
was. Monday would have seemed like the behaviour
of a man in love—which he wasn't. Tuesday, ditto.
Thursday would have made her seem like an after-
thought and Friday an insult.

So Wednesday it was.

'Kiloran?'

'Hi!'

His voice was soft. 'How are you?'

Imagine if she told him the truth—that she had
spent the last three days worrying that he wasn't going

to ring at all! 'I'm fine,' she said lightly. 'How's the new job?'

'Busy.'

'Oh.' She waited.

'Going to come up to London and see me this weekend?'

'You don't want to come down here?'

'Can't. I have a big, glitzy ball to attend on Saturday night—it's a work-related thing and I wondered if you might like to be my guest?'

She gave it just the right amount of consideration. 'I'd love to.'

There was a pause. 'And you'll stay?'

'If you like.'

Adam gave a wry smile. She certainly wasn't over-eager. 'I'd like that very much,' he said evenly. 'Let me give you my address.'

Kiloran felt stricken with nerves as she drove to London on Saturday evening, having tried on about seven dresses before finally deciding on the one she had started with.

Adam's flat was in Kensington—the first two floors of a period town house in one of the smartest roads.

He opened the door to her knock, looking nothing short of devastating, even though his dark hair was still damp from the shower and the snowy shirt, which contrasted with black, tapered trousers, wasn't buttoned up.

Kiloran's nervousness increased tenfold as his eyes narrowed. Maybe all the other women would be wearing long and she would be the only one in a knee-skimmer? Would it have seemed gauche and naïve to have checked with him first?

She smoothed her hand down over a silver-silk-clad hip. 'Will this do?'

'Do?' He pulled her into his arms and resisted the temptation to let his hand slowly travel the same route, because if he started doing *that*, then they would never get out of the door.

She looked as exquisite as some cool, gleaming moonstone, with not a hair on her shiny blonde head out of place. He liked the don't-touch-me air—the contrast between the ice-queen of now and the fire-cracker she would later become. 'Oh, yes, you'll *do*. In fact, you look so gorgeous that I imagine I'll have to chain you to my side all night.' He smiled and dropped a light kiss on her lips. 'Mmm. Better not spoil your lipstick. Come and talk to me while I finish getting ready and then I'll pour you a drink.'

It was an urbane and sophisticated line but this was not what Kiloran wanted at all. She would have preferred if he had dragged her straight upstairs and rav-ished her to within an inch of her life—but she couldn't just rely on sex to stop her feeling insecure, could she? She had fallen for the urbane and sophis-ticated man—so she could hardly start complaining that he wasn't acting like a caveman!

'That sounds lovely,' she said calmly and followed him through to a large, airy sitting room. There were squashy sofas and restful water colours on the walls and a bottle of pink champagne stood cooling in an ice bucket.

'I'll just get my tie.'

She nodded, watching while he went into the bedroom, where he picked up a bow-tie and began deftly knotting it.

He could see her reflection in the mirror as she looked around the sitting room. 'Like it?'

She turned her head towards the sound of his voice and she could see that the bed was invitingly yet dauntingly vast and there were fresh flowers beside it. But he wasn't asking about the bedroom and so she concentrated on the view over the square in the sitting room instead. 'It's lovely. Peaceful and pretty.'

'Isn't it? I'm only renting until I decide where to buy. This is on the market, but I don't know whether it would be big enough.'

For what? For a resolutely single man who had the occasional visiting girlfriend? She focussed like mad on a tree, aware that if she spent the whole time concentrating on how completely separate their lives were, then it wouldn't work at all. And this was only the beginning, for heaven's sake.

He finished knotting the tie and came into the sitting room, and Kiloran's stomach flipped. If there was any chaining to do, then she imagined it would be entirely mutual.

'Shall we have a glass of champagne? There's a car collecting us at seven.'

'Yes, please.' They were, she realised, acting as if they had just met. And why hadn't he kissed her properly—lipstick or no damned lipstick?

He popped the cork, poured two glasses and handed her one. 'What shall we drink to?'

'Success?'

He shook his head. 'No. To beauty.' His eyes glittered with unspoken promise. 'To you, Kiloran,' he said softly, and chinked his glass against hers.

The compliment made her feel quite dizzy, and the wine, taken on an empty stomach, only added to it, but at least it relaxed the knot in her stomach a little bit. 'Why, thank you,' she murmured.

The ball was predictably glamorous and there was a giant ice sculpture of an eagle, keeping pounds of finest beluga caviar at just the right temperature.

'Slightly over the top,' whispered Adam as he guided her by the elbow to their table.

So were most of the women—wearing dresses which made her own feel positively understated. Some of the women gave her openly envious looks and Kiloran was glad that Adam was newly arrived back from the States—she would have hated to have been classified as girlfriend number twenty-two.

She played her part of sophisticated partner to the full. She chatted animatedly and laughed at jokes—some funny, some not. She delicately but politely fended off the advances of a senior banking figure who had been hitting the bottle hard for most of the evening.

Adam watched her, a pulse beating steadily at his temple. She had barely looked at him all evening and the novelty factor of that was driving him crazy. Not that he needed any added incentives. He glanced at his watch surreptitiously.

'Kiloran?'

She looked up, caught in the crossfire of his grey eyes. 'Mmm?'

'Ready to go home now?'

'Sure.'

In the darkened seclusion of the car, he drew her into his arms as he had wanted to do all evening, drinking in her perfume and revelling in the softness of her skin. 'God, that evening dragged, didn't it?'

With his lips on her neck it was hard to think about anything, but she maintained the demure air of the corporate companion. 'I rather enjoyed it.'

'Did you?' He slipped his hand beneath her coat to cup her silver-satined breast, his mouth against her hair as he whispered, 'Tell me what else you enjoy, honey.'

And it was madness itself on the one hand to have wished that he had kissed her instead of talking to her at the beginning of the evening, and then to wish that he would talk to her now instead of kissing her! What the hell did she want from the man?

Kiloran gave up thinking—it was much easier to go under the spell of his kiss and slip into a relationship which gave her some, though certainly not all, of what she wanted.

Weekdays separated them—they met on Friday and parted on Sunday. Sometimes Adam came down to Lacey's, but more often than not Kiloran went up to London, where Adam wanted to rediscover the city he had left behind eight years earlier. And Kiloran found herself seeing a different city from the one she was used to, because she saw it through Adam's eyes as well as her own, and it slowly crept up on her that they were the eyes of a woman falling in love.

At first she tried to deny it, and then to talk herself out of it, asking whether it was possible to fall in love if it was very definitely one-sided. But it was. Of course it was. Unrequited love—the biggest heart-breaker in history and as old as time itself.

She was headachey one Sunday evening, when she was driving back to Lacey's, having just spent a sat-isfying yet ultimately dissatisfying weekend at the flat. There had been a dinner on Saturday, a lazy Sunday morning in bed, then the papers and brunch and a walk in the park. They had gone back to bed and then the telephone had rung and Adam had been speaking to someone in America, and Kiloran had slipped out of bed to shower and wondered whether he had even no-ticed her going.

She found herself wondering about the natural term of his relationships, and wondered, if she finished it, how long it would take him to replace her with some-one else whom she found as attractive. And why was she even thinking about finishing it, when to all intents and purposes it was the perfect relationship?

Perfect like a diamond—glittering yet cold.

And that was Adam. His charm could not disguise the fact that he was a man who viewed any kind of commitment as he would a deadly cobra.

She had been looking at a huge, double-page spread in one of the Sunday glossies, all about the Caribbean.

'Doesn't that look blissful?' she questioned, her finger stabbing at white, bleached sand and sea the colour of crystal peacock.

He looked up from the financial section, more captivated by her green eyes than any damned beach. 'Mmm?'

'This. Look.'

He glanced down at it. 'Very pretty.'

'Have you ever been to the Caribbean?'

'Once. A long time ago.'

Getting information about his past was like getting blood out of a stone and for once—just for the hell of it—Kiloran decided to ignore the I-don't-particularly-want-to-talk-about-it vibes.

'When?'

He put the newspaper down. 'About five years ago.'

'Who with?'

His face became shuttered. 'I'm sorry?'

She was hardly demanding to know all the secrets to his heart! 'I just asked who with.' And then rushed on incautiously. 'Was it with a woman?'

Now he really *was* starting to get irritated. 'Why?'

'No reason, especially.' Kiloran shrugged, feeling on the defensive. 'It's just—'

His eyes glittered. 'Just what, Kiloran?'

'Well, it's quite interesting to know about other people you've been out with. Don't you think?'

'No, I don't. I have no earthly desire to find out when you went out with Johnny, or Dickie, or Harry—

or whoever else might be clogging up the romantic files in your memory. Why should I?'

Why, indeed? His voice sounded cold, clipped—she hadn't heard it sound like that in all the time she had been going out with him.

But something made her probe away—with the poorly applied knowledge of someone who continued to pick a spot: that it always left a scar.

'It's called wanting to get to know someone better, Adam.'

His eyes gleamed out an unspoken warning. 'Or intrusion, perhaps?' he questioned easily, getting up from his chair and going to stand behind her, his fingers beginning to rhythmically massage her shoulders. 'I know everything I want to know about you, Miss Lacey.'

She closed her eyes as she felt her body respond to his touch. Instantly turned on by him and furious with herself for being so. She tipped her head back, so that she caught the upside-down version of his face, and from this angle his features were distorted.

'You can't keep relationships in aspic,' she objected.

He sighed, and stopped what he was doing. 'I told you right from the beginning what this relationship was likely to entail, Kiloran,' he said shortly. 'You knew where you stood and you agreed to that, didn't you?'

She nodded. He made it sound like a business merger.

His voice softened. 'Do you enjoy being with me, or not?'

Did the sun rise in the skies every morning? She nodded again.

'Well, then—don't let's spoil it.'

She didn't say anything.

He looked at the frozen set of her shoulders. Why could women never be satisfied with the status quo? Why, if there was a boat drifting along on perfectly calm and pleasant waters, did they always want to rock it? Well, let her sulk if she wanted to sulk! 'I'm going to take a shower,' he said shortly.

And that had been that. She had been left feeling foolish, frustrated, and wishing that she had kept her mouth shut, but on the drive home she questioned whether their so-called relationship could continue like this. Relationships had to grow, didn't they—or they withered and died?

Maybe that was what Adam wanted. Natural wastage.

He rang on Thursday to say that he had to fly to Rome. 'And I won't be back until late Saturday.'

'But you were supposed to be coming down to see me!' She knew as she was saying it that she was playing it all wrong, but that didn't seem to stop her and, besides, why *should* it be a game?

'I know I was—but there isn't really going to be enough time.' A look of determination came over his face. She had to accept what he was offering her, because he wasn't going to offer more than that. 'Let's leave it this time, Kiloran, shall we?'

It seemed she didn't have any say in the matter. 'Fine,' she agreed, resolutely cheerful and yet somehow despising herself.

His voice softened. 'Listen, I'll come down next weekend and make it up to you. How about that?'

But she felt like a child being fobbed off with an inferior toy at Christmas.

She had thought that she would just love being with Adam so much that she would be prepared to go along with the kind of grown-up relationship he had outlined right at the start.

But she was slowly beginning to realise that it wasn't enough—and if it wasn't enough *now*, then what did the future hold?

Adam did what he always did when emotions began to wreak their usual havoc—he buried himself in his work, winning two deals which made him the toast of his new offices.

Success was just as heady as power—for the onlookers, at least, he decided. Two senior female executives had been fawning over him all morning and the more stunning of the two had invited him for a drink after work.

He wasn't remotely tempted. He was tired and he thought of Kiloran, with her grass-green eyes and her fall of moon-coloured hair and a body which took him to places he hadn't realised existed.

And then he remembered the ugly little scene on Sunday.

'I'm pretty tied up at the moment,' he prevaricated. 'I'm completely into rain checks,' smiled the executive, and popped her card into the jacket of his suit. 'Let me know when you're free.'

Rome was crowded and the man he was dealing with a complete incompetent. By the time he arrived in the UK on Saturday evening, Adam had a splitting headache which was not helped by the fact that the airline seemed to have misplaced his bag.

The pretty ground stewardess smiled at him anxiously. 'If you'd like to wait—'

'I've been waiting at the airport for two hours,' said Adam, trying to keep his voice steady. It wasn't *her* fault, after all. 'Just have them send it to me, will you?'

'Certainly, sir.'

To cap it all, it was raining—a driving, relentless rain and he felt full of a pent-up kind of anger, unable to pinpoint the cause of it.

He got into his car, half expecting it not to start, but the powerful engine roared into life immediately and he thought about driving back to London, to an empty flat and an empty bed.

And then he thought about Kiloran and his body responded as instantly as the car had done.

Hadn't he been a little harsh with her?

What if he drove down to see her—surprised her— gave her the perfume he'd bought her in Rome? And then spent the rest of the weekend lost in her arms?

Anticipation caused his face to tighten as he indicated left out of the airport, instead of right.

The drive was one of the worst of his life. The narrow lanes were clogged with mud and the hedgerows seemed to be closing in on him. The radio was playing some loud and intense choral piece which seemed to darken his mood even more and Adam automatically clicked it off, so that for a moment there was silence.

Only a moment.

A car came suddenly in the other direction, hidden until that moment by a sharp bend. Adam's powerful headlights illuminated the vehicle and for just a moment he saw a man driving, one hand on the wheel, the other holding a mobile phone to his ear.

The car was coming towards him. Adam slammed on his brakes and jammed his fist on the horn and his car slowed right down, but it was too late, because the other just kept on coming.

As if in slow motion, Adam saw a frightened, startled face staring at him through the windscreen of the other car and then a loud crash, a jolt of pain.

And then, thankfully, nothing.

CHAPTER TEN

THE telephone rang at midnight, waking Kiloran from a deep and troubled sleep, and she sat up with a start, glancing at the bedside clock in alarm and wondering who would be ringing at this time of the night, and why.

Was it Grandfather?

She snatched the receiver up. 'Hello?'

It was a man's voice, a voice she did not recognise, a low, husky voice. 'Is this Kiloran Lacey?'

'That's me. Who is this, please?'

'This is the police.'

Kiloran began to shake. The *police*?

'Are you a friend of Adam Black's?'

Something in the way he asked the question alerted every fearful instinct in Kiloran's body. It was as though someone had constricted her throat with a tight metal band.

'I'm his…yes,' she struggled the words out. 'He's a friend of mine. Something's happened to him, hasn't it?' she managed to get out.

'Yes. I'm afraid that he's been involved in a car crash. He's been badly hurt.'

Kiloran gave a little moan of distress, her fingers gripping onto the receiver as if it were a lifeline.

'Yours was the last number he had dialled on his mobile and—'

'Adam!' It sounded like the keening wail of a wounded animal. Kiloran's hands began to shake. 'Where is he?'

'In hospital. The Tremaine Hospital—it's near you—do you know it?'

'Yes.'

'Are you all right to drive, or would you rather we send a car round for you?'

'No. No—I can manage. Th-thank you.' Kiloran slammed the phone down and jumped out of bed, grabbing a pair of old jeans and the warmest sweater she could find, her fingers shaking so much that she could barely do her bra up.

Calm down, she told herself. For God's sake, calm down, or you'll end up crashing your own car. A jolt of pain ripped through her. Just how badly hurt was he?

She forced herself to drive at an exaggeratedly slow pace all the way to Tremaine Hospital, but she left her car skewed in the hospital forecourt and ran into the reception as if the hounds of hell were snapping at her ankles.

'Can you tell me where Adam Black is, please?'

'When was he admitted?'

'I don't *know*!'

'Just a moment.' The woman ran her eyes down a list and then looked up, her face folded into a deliberately calm expression. 'He's in the intensive care unit, he—'

But Kiloran had already gone, taking the stairs instead of the lift, running all the way to the isolated and sterile unit right at the very top of the hospital wing.

A nurse in a white uniform looked up from the desk. 'May I help you?'

She felt like crying that it wasn't *her* that needed help, but Adam—but she took a deep breath. Hysteria would help no one. She must be strong. 'I've come to see Adam Black.'

'Are you a relative?'

'No.' She wanted to say, I'm all he's got, but that wasn't true, not in the real sense. 'I'm his girlfriend. He has no next of kin.'

'I see.' The nurse got to her feet. 'If you'd like to wait here for a moment.'

The moment felt like eternity but eventually the nurse came back with a colleague.

'My name is Sandy,' she said gently. 'And I am Adam's nurse. Won't you sit down for a moment and I'll tell you what is happening with him?'

Another moment. Another eternity. Kiloran forced herself to concentrate.

He was concussed. He was in a coma. There didn't appear to be any major internal injuries and he had just undergone a brain scan. The good news was that he hadn't broken any limbs.

That was the *good* news?

Kiloran gave a ghostly smile. 'When can I see him?'

'I'll take you to him now.'

It was like some surreal nightmare as she followed

the nurse through the spotless, soundless and gleaming unit until they finally stopped outside a cubicle.

Through the glass, Kiloran could see Adam lying as still as death on the bed and she jammed her fist into her mouth and gave a soundless little cry. Her Adam— her strong, powerful Adam—with all that vitality just zapped away.

'What can I do?' she whispered. 'To help him?'

'Talk to him. Stroke his hand. Remind him of things you've done together. Try to bring him back.'

Remind him of things you've done together. The words haunted her as she fearfully made her way towards the bed, towards that still and silent figure.

What shared memories did they have which might stir his sleeping mind? But the only ones she could think of were not the deep and meaningful memories which would arouse a man from a coma. Great sex and glitzy restaurants were not the kind of profound or precious memories which would arouse the sleeping mind. Were they?

She could, of course, say that she loved the way that his mouth sometimes softened when he was about to kiss her. Or that it felt as if she had just won a prize if something she said made him laugh aloud. Or that when he was sleeping she could see the boy in the face of the man and that he could look almost vulnerable.

But not this time. She flinched as she looked at the bruised and battered face. There was no vulnerability in Adam's face today. It was barely recognisable as a face—man or boy—it was so distorted and discoloured with bruising. And besides, those were not the kinds of things he wanted to hear, not from her and not from any woman.

So what the hell was she going to say to him?

She sat down beside the bed and began to stroke his hand. What did he like most about her? He liked the strong and in-control Kiloran, and that was what she would be.

She took a deep breath and smiled at the nurse. 'Adam Black,' she said, very softly. 'You are nothing but an old attention-seeker! I've been woken up out of a deep sleep to come and see you, and you haven't even the decency to open your eyes and say hello.' And then her voice cracked just a little. Oh, what the hell? 'Wake up, Adam,' she pleaded softly. 'Wake up, darling.'

For nearly two days he lay there while the nurses turned him and washed him and took his observations.

And for nearly two days Kiloran remained by his side, except when they forced her to go and rest in the small side room especially reserved for 'relatives'.

It was when the sun was going down on the second day that he finally stirred.

Kiloran had been talking to him, still in the new, soft voice which she seemed to have specially acquired for this heartbreakingly one-way conversation.

'The business rooms are fully booked for the next six months,' she was saying. 'And the weirdest thing of all is that someone spotted the photos of the garden and showed them to an expert, and *he* said that he had never seen such a big collection of unusual shrubs and trees. And—'

She drew a deep breath and wistfully stroked the back of his hand, remembering a snapshot image of the day the two of them had stood in the garden, that first day he had come to work at Lacey's. They had been bathed in sunlight and Adam had looked so strong—as if he were the most alive person on the planet. And then he had told her about his mother, about Vaughn giving him the job. Knowing him now, as she did—or what little he allowed her to know— she realised that it had been a strangely intimate thing for him to have told her. Never to be repeated.

'And some terribly up-market magazine wants to do a feature on it! Imagine! They especially loved the lily collection, and you know your favourite—the pink and white one? They want to put that on the cover!'

Through the heavy grey mists of a wasteland he seemed to have inhabited since the beginning of time, Adam heard a soft, sweet voice talking of lilies and he thought he had died and gone to heaven.

He tried to move his mouth.

'Nurse!' Kiloran stumbled to her feet and knocked the chair over. *'Nurse!'* She bent over him. 'Adam— oh, *Adam*! Darling, can you hear me?'

Something, or someone had superglued his eyes together, but with an almighty effort Adam forced them open by a fraction, but such a fierce and piercing light scorched them that he let them snap shut again.

'Nurse—he tried to open his eyes—I swear he did!' Nurse? *Nurse?*

'Just move aside for a minute, would you, Kiloran?'

Kiloran? Was that a name, for God's sake? Or some kind of mountain? His mind fuddled along.

'Come along, Mr Black—try to open your eyes for me!'

A voice infinitely less soft and sweet was speaking to him again. A bossy kind of voice. 'Come along, Mr Black—open your eyes.'

With an effort, he obeyed—only to have Bossy-voice shine some God-forsaken light in them. If he could have groaned, he would have done, but his vocal cords seemed to have let him down.

'Yes, he's conscious.'

'Oh, thank God! Thank *God*!'

Sweet-voice sounded close to tears—a sound so poignant that he wrenched his eyes open. A beautiful face was staring down at him, with hair the colour of sunlight and green eyes that swam like the ocean. It was all too confusing and Adam let himself slip gratefully back into that grey wasteland.

CHAPTER ELEVEN

'SO HOW are we feeling this morning, Adam?'

Adam opened his eyes. 'Where's Kiloran?'

The nurse smiled. Men were a bit like animals—if the first thing a duck saw was a tiger, then it forever believed that the tiger was its mother! And Kiloran, in this case—was the tiger!

'Kiloran's just bringing the car round to the front of the building—and I'm here to help you get dressed.'

'I can get myself dressed!'

'Not yet, you can't,' the nurse fussed. 'You're as weak as a kitten, although I must say that you don't particularly *look* as weak as a kitten!'

'Why can't Kiloran help me?' he demanded, his heart sinking as he saw the nurse begin to roll her sleeves up over her rather hefty forearms. He'd much rather that golden-haired angel be at hand.

The nurse coughed. 'Well, she was a little taken-aback when you didn't recognise her, of course—but, as I told her, that's perfectly normal in these circumstances.'

'You mean I know her?'

The nurse helped him on with his jeans and began to get rather pink around the neck.

'Yes, Adam,' said Kiloran, in an odd, strained kind

of voice as she walked into the cubicle. 'You do know me—you just can't remember.'

Adam was still feeling groggy, but not too groggy to wonder how well he had known her.

'Here.' Kiloran began to slide a sweater over his head, her fingers automatically colliding with the silken flesh, and she saw him still, their eyes meeting, his full of confusion, and something else, too—some fleeting look of sensual awareness.

Kiloran would have been shocked if she hadn't already noticed Adam's body responding in the most elemental way possible—even when he'd been deeply unconscious.

It had happened on the second morning, when she had been helping the nurse to wash him. It had been a little embarrassing—for Kiloran, in any case.

But as the nurse had cheerfully explained, 'Oh, I wouldn't worry about *that*, my dear! Men are very basic creatures. They would need to be at death's door before their bodies stopped reacting.' She withdrew the sponge hastily from his chest. 'It's an automatic response,' she added hastily. 'It's not me, or anything.'

Kiloran had managed to smile. The nurse in question was of pensionable age and although she was very sweet—she did not imagine that she was really Adam's type.

But now, the look she surprised in his eyes was not simply an automatic masculine response to the touch of a young woman, of that she was certain. There had been the glimmer of memory there, she would have sworn it.

Did that mean he was starting to remember?

Because up until now, his mind had been a complete blank. He seemed to recognise his own name, but that was all. He didn't know why he had been driving so near to Kiloran's when he had specifically told her that he was going straight home to his apartment. Nor did he have any knowledge of any relationship between the two of them.

Though that, accepted Kiloran wryly, might say more about the definition of their 'relationship' than any memory loss.

And she was taking him back to Lacey's, assured by the medical team that he needed only rest and recuperation and not any high-powered nursing care. All of which she was perfectly capable of administering.

She wanted to do it; she loved him, but she knew that even if she hadn't she would have done it, anyway—for who else did he have?

That had been the most profound shock of all—of realising that such a strong and powerful man was, after all, as vulnerable as the next person.

'Let me help you—' She moved to help his arms into the sweater, but he tried to push her away.

'I can do it—'

'No, you can't! Are you always this stubborn, Adam?'

'No, honey—you're the one who's stubb—'

Their eyes met in a long look. He had called her 'honey' and he had called her...

'Yes, that's right,' she said slowly. 'I *am* stubborn.'

'You mean that's memory?' he demanded, as if he

had just discovered the secret to the universe. 'Not guesswork?'

She smiled. 'It certainly seems that way. Now stop worrying about it, about anything—I'm going to take you home.'

'You're bossier than that nurse,' he complained, but he was wondering exactly where home was.

It was not what he imagined it would be—a huge and beautiful mansion, set in acres of exquisite grounds.

'This is where I live?' he questioned as the car crunched its way up the gravelled drive.

'Some of the time,' she replied evenly, because the doctor had told her to simplify things. And he *did* spend weekends there, with her, some of the time.

'With you?'

She nodded. 'Yes, with me—though we don't live together, as such.'

He wondered why. Through eyes newly focussed on the brightness of life after the greyness of his coma, he thought that he had never seen a more beautiful woman than Kiloran.

'You have an apartment in London,' she went on, staring at him for some kind of recognition. 'In Kensington.' But there was none—nothing other than the blank kind of acceptance which greeted each new fact which she recounted. It made her realise how many subtle interpretations of a 'fact' there could be. If you told someone that you spent weekends together, it could sound like quite a commitment—while nothing, of course, could be further from the truth. Not that Adam was into subtle nuances right now.

'Come on, now,' she said gently, thinking how much she wanted to use a term of endearment, like 'sweetheart' or 'darling'—but that was something she had only done when he'd been in a coma and she hadn't been able to help herself. And now was very definitely not the time to carry on with it. She was supposed to be helping his memory to return by keeping things much as they'd been before the accident. And besides, the doctor hoped that the amnesia would only be temporary—imagine Adam's icy horror if his memory suddenly returned, to find her acting lovesick all over him!

'You're very tired,' she whispered, slipping her arm around his waist as she took in the dark shadows beneath his eyes and the lines of fraught tension on his face.

Some autopilot reaction made him try to push her arm away. 'I'm fine.'

She ignored him, knowing that he didn't have the strength to resist. She tightened her grip on him and reluctantly he leaned on her as they went into the house.

She had asked Miriam to bring tea and crumpets and buns to the library, where a fire had been lit and was roaring. She had wanted the most English of teas to see if that would nudge some kind of memory, because they'd sometimes had tea in here, just like this, after riding. She shot him a glance to see his reaction.

He looked around the room, taking in the very cosy

scene in front of his eyes. It felt as though someone had muzzled his brain with cotton wool and he shook his head in irritation as he sank down into a chair in front of the fire.

'How would you like your tea, Adam?' asked Kiloran, lifting up the heavy silver pot.

'Just lemon, please,' he replied automatically and saw her smile. 'What is it?'

'That's how you always take your tea.'

'So my brain is sorting out the most important things, right?' he questioned drily and she smiled again.

'At least your sense of humour hasn't completely deserted you.'

'You mean I have one?'

'Sometimes.' She was about to tease him when she drew herself up short. 'Don't tire him,' the doctor had told her—and perhaps teasing would qualify as tiring him. 'Have a sandwich.'

He shook his head. 'I'm not hungry.'

She nodded. She wasn't going to force it, but he looked so pale, so unlike her glowing Adam that if she could have persuaded him to eat she would have done. 'Okay.'

Adam drank his tea. It was very comfortable here by the fire—warm and welcoming. If only his head didn't feel as though someone had jammed it in between a giant nutcracker, and in the process managed to take away all the thoughts and associations and familiarity which made him what he normally was.

But how did he know what he normally was?

He put the cup down and looked at Kiloran, which was halfway to a cure in itself. She was wearing a soft wool dress, the colour of blueberries, and her hair was loose—like the moon against the backdrop of a nearly dark sky. Her long, slim legs were spread in front of her and she had kicked her shoes off. He might be only two days out of a coma, but that didn't mean that *all* his senses were dead. He might have a little difficulty wanting food as he usually did, but the stirring leap of awareness and the pounding of his heart made him thank God that a very important part of him was still very much alive.

'Kiloran?'

She had seen him watching her, studying her in a way she had not seen him do before, except perhaps when they'd been in bed together. Never usually that openly. His eyes had darkened and suddenly she was reminded of how long it had been since they had made love. 'What?' she said huskily.

For a moment, he almost forgot the question, but with a steely determination he dragged it back out of the reach of growing desire. This was too important to wait. He would not forget anything else; he had forgotten enough. And then it occurred to him that his ability to make love might have been affected. His mouth hardened. Like hell it would! 'How would you describe me? Normally?'

Kiloran saw the perplexing pattern of emotions which had flitted across his gorgeous face—expressions she had never seen there before. There had been uncertainty and concern and then the familiar steely resolve. 'Six-two, black hair—'

'Not the way I look—hell, Kiloran! I can see in the mirror and have enough imagination to realise that my face isn't usually black and blue and swollen to twice its size! I mean, how would you describe me—the man. If you're my lover, then you must know me better than anyone else.'

The irony of his remark didn't escape her. If she told him that she suspected no one *really*, *really* knew him, because he always kept something of himself back—then would that sound like a criticism? And what right did she have to criticise him? She loved him, didn't she, in spite of that? She couldn't make him into a more emotionally giving person just because that suited her template of what her true-love should be. You couldn't control the way someone was, or adapt them to suit your fantasies.

'What kind of a person are you?' she mused. 'Well, you're very hard-working. And disciplined. And focussed. You're very successful—one of the top five investment bankers in the world, probably. People respect you—'

'You make me sound like a machine,' he said, and a note of something like bitterness crept into his voice.

Her voice softened. 'Oh, you're no machine, Adam—I can assure you of that.' She drew a deep breath, because this kind of thing wasn't easy to say, out cold, from the other side of the room—to a man who technically was your lover but who didn't remember a thing about you. 'You're a warm, giving lover.' She swallowed. 'The best lover I've ever had.'

As a testimony it was curiously lacking, and his mind was too tired and too befuddled to put his finger on exactly what it was.

Kiloran rose to her feet, an anxious look on her face. 'You've tired yourself out. You need to rest—'

'I'm not a damned invalid—'

'Well, yes, Adam,' she said firmly, coming to stand over him, a stern expression on her face. 'Actually, you are at the moment. And if you want to get better, you're going to have to do exactly as I say. The doctor told me to tell you that.'

'And if I refuse?'

'Then I'll hire a nurse to look after you. Someone like Sandy.'

He shuddered as he remembered Bossy-voice and imagined just how much *she* would crack the whip. He stared at Kiloran. There was something awfully appealing about such an ethereal-looking beauty coming on to him like a school-marm, but something here definitely did not compute. The felt curtain across his mind twitched by just a fraction. 'I'm not used to being told what to do by you, am I?'

She shook her head. 'Not by me, not by anyone.'

'Am I a tyrant, Kiloran?'

For a moment she forgot that he was an invalid. 'I'm not the kind of person who would go out with a tyrant,' she said drily. 'No matter how gorgeous he happened to be.'

'So you think I'm gorgeous, do you?'

It was, she realised, the first time that she had ever dared tell him *anything* about the way she felt. 'You aren't bad,' she said grudgingly. 'When your face isn't bruised and battered.'

He laughed. 'And I'm definitely not a tyrant?'

She pretended to consider this. 'Out of ten on the tyrannical scale, you would score a fairly modest rating of three.' She took a deep breath. He seemed to want to hear the truth, so surely she should give it to him.

'You're master of your own kingdom, Adam,' she said slowly. 'That's all. You live life entirely on your own terms.'

'Doesn't everyone?'

'Maybe not to such a great extent.'

He wanted to ask her more. Like why—but an overwhelming lassitude had started to seep into his bones. He closed his eyes and yawned.

'Now you really *are* going to bed,' she said severely.

The eyes flew open and there was a mocking look glinting in their depths which made Kiloran's heart turn over. Come back to me, Adam, she pleaded silently. Please come back to me.

Until the awful thought occurred to her that this new Adam was infinitely softer, more malleable, and far easier to relate to.

What if the old Adam came back and she found that

she was no longer prepared to cope with the relationship on the old terms?

But that was jumping ahead a step too far.

'Bedtime,' she said unsteadily.

For the next couple of days Adam recuperated, using the most powerful method of recuperation which existed.

He slept. For hours and hours at a time, tucked up in Kiloran's big four-poster bed.

The first time she had taken him up there, she had watched him carefully, to see if there was some kind of reaction, some recognition that they had indulged in so many pleasures of the senses here in this room.

But there had been none. No stirring of memory— though that did not mean that he'd been indifferent to the bed. No way. He had laconically raised his dark eyebrows over tired eyes.

'Going to join me, Kiloran?' he yawned.

Kiloran bent her head to pull back the duvet, not wanting him to see any trace of vulnerability, or sadness. What she wouldn't have given to have climbed in beside him, wrapped her naked body next to his and hugged him tight. Not wanting sex from him, just closeness and wanting to give him comfort in return.

But she could not envisage a scenario where they went to bed without making love—it was not that kind of relationship. Adam loved sex. Well, so did she, for that matter—especially with him—but sometimes she found herself wishing for the intimacy which came *without* having sex.

Not for them the lazy familiarity which came from being totally relaxed in each other's company. There had always been reservations, barriers between them. Her wishing he would let his guard down and him always being wary of giving too much away.

And although their relationship had been satisfying—there had never, not once, been a shared vision of a future together. With Adam it had never been more than what they had today. And while that made her appreciate what she *had* got, it also made her long for what she had not. Commitment—and that was one thing she would never get from him.

'I'll sleep next door for the time being. I think you need a little space,' she said lightly.

And so did she.

He pulled a face of objection, but he was too tired to object too much. He lay down on the bed and it felt like heaven.

'Okay,' he yawned. 'If you say so.'

But within a couple of weeks he began to show very definite signs of improvement—physically, at least. The sleep showed in the renewed brightening of his eyes and the familiar healthy glow of his skin. Often she took him outside, to sit in the restorative spring sunshine and to sit quietly in the haven which the garden provided. He was eating proper meals, too—the freshest, most delicious food that Kiloran could conjure up.

She put two plates of salmon down on the table one evening and a dish of new potatoes, and crunchy, bright green mange-tout. He smiled. 'Mmm. Who cooked this?'

'I did.'

The curtain twitched. 'But…you don't cook,' he said slowly.

She looked up from spooning a potato onto her plate. 'No, that's right. I didn't used to cook,' she agreed calmly.

'But you do now?'

'That's right. I quite like it, actually.'

'So what changed?'

She knew and he knew that they weren't in the remotest bit interested in her culinary conversion. This was a scent on the trail to recall. A trail that she yearned to complete and yet dreaded at the same time. 'You changed me.'

'*I* did?'

'Uh-huh.'

He stared at her, thinking how exquisitely pure the black velvet dress made her look. 'I complained?'

She shook her head. 'Not really. But you were obviously disapproving of the fact that I had servants and let them take care of me.'

He nodded, digesting this. So she had sought his approval, had she? Now why was that? 'Kiloran,' he said suddenly, and something in his voice made her go very still.

'Yes, Adam?'

'Just how do I know you?'

CHAPTER TWELVE

KILORAN put the spoon down with a hand which had suddenly begun to tremble and stared at Adam.

'How do I know you?' he repeated.

The doctor had told her this might happen; she was only surprised that it hadn't happened sooner. He had said that Adam's mind might naturally fill in some or all of the gaps by itself. Or that he might require assistance to do so.

The challenge was going to be telling him the truth. In confronting reality, however painful. For she was astute enough to recognise that by telling him this particular story, she would automatically give away a lot of her own feelings, if she was going to be brutally honest.

And that might frighten him.

'We met when my grandfather asked you to come and help our ailing business,' she said succinctly.

'How long ago?' he shot out.

She frowned. 'Almost nine months ago,' she said. Heavens above—was it really that long? And how ironic. It was longer than she had realised and yet it also seemed a ridiculously short time. But a human embryo could grow into full and sustainable life in exactly that time. 'Though I had actually met you years before.'

Now it was his turn to frown. 'When?'

'You worked here when you were eighteen,' she explained slowly. 'You grew up around here.'

'What about my mother?' he demanded. 'And father?'

Now she was in the most terrible dilemma. He had confided in her the truth about his background back at the beginning, back in that sunlit garden, which now seemed like a lifetime ago.

Could he take hearing this? Something which he normally chose to suppress.

'Keep nothing back,' the doctor had urged.

'But what if it's painful?' had been her response.

'The past often is, Miss Lacey. So is life. Protect against pain and there is no growth. And without growth, we die.'

'You never knew your father, Adam. And you haven't seen your mother since that summer, all those years ago.'

The felt curtain which was blocking recall now blew gently as a dark wind began to whisper across his mind. He was taken back to a morning long ago. A kitchen. Unwashed dishes in the sink and a note on the table. She wasn't coming back. She had gone. Gone and taken something with her. His hopes and his dreams and, unless he did something about it—his reputation.

Adam flinched and stared at her, his eyes dark with pain. 'I remember,' he said slowly. 'I remember. The house. The emptiness.' There was a long, raw pause. 'My mother had gone.'

She heard the finality in his voice and moved so that she was close enough to touch him, close enough to grip his forearm as if willing him to bring it all back to mind. 'But what else do you remember, Adam? What else?'

He shook his head. It was like swimming in cloudy water. Sometimes the light appeared on the surface, but then once again the mud obscured it. He stared into her green, green eyes and let his gaze travel down to lips as soft and as luscious as ripe strawberries.

And suddenly he did not want the past—he wanted the present, with all its infinitely more pleasurable associations. Why elect for pain when this beautiful woman was touching him, reminding him with dizzying recall just how wonderful pleasure could be? 'Kiss me, Kiloran,' he said softly.

She shook her head. 'Not now. It's too soon.'

'Kiss me,' he repeated, and something of his old mastery returned.

She moved her face closer, frozen in that position for one breathtaking moment, their eyes locked in glittering question. At that moment she had never felt closer to him.

'Now,' he murmured.

She lowered her lips onto his. A tender brush which became a tiny kiss. She felt his sigh warm against her and their lips parted by a fraction, melding in a sweet, exploratory kiss which felt like two teenagers trying one out for the first time.

It felt as if she had never really kissed him before, Kiloran thought with a jolt, and her breath quickened.

He reached his hand up to touch her neck, wonderingly, as if he had never felt skin before, but in a way he hadn't. His senses had needed to die in that coma to spring to life as never before. The heavy throb of desire beat its silken heat in his blood, but for once there was no urgency to consummate. He wanted to make this last all night.

He drew his mouth away. 'Let's go to bed.'

She shook her head, her heart thundering. 'You aren't well enough.'

'Says who?'

'I don't know what the doctor would say—'

'Damn the doctor!' He scraped his chair back and took her hand.

'Adam, we mustn't.'

'Kiloran,' he said simply. 'We can't not.'

She felt her cheeks flame, for the words seemed like an avowal of something she had long hoped for, until she reminded herself that they weren't. They were a declaration of fact. And of intent. His body and his mind had been very nearly lifeless, and now they wanted to celebrate life itself in the most basic way possible. Just as his hunger had returned to help him heal, so too had another, different kind of hunger.

'Okay,' she agreed softly. 'Bed it is.'

She felt as shy as a virgin bride on her wedding night as he took her by the hand and led her upstairs, walking like a man who had never known a day's sickness in his life, let alone one whose life had, just a few weeks earlier, been hanging on by a thread.

The bedroom door closed behind them, Adam took

her into his arms, bending his head so that his mouth was very close to hers. 'What do you like me to do best?' he asked softly.

'Kiss me,' she murmured.

He needed no second bidding, groaning as he sweetly plundered her lips, on and on and on, as if the kiss were a fountain of life and he were drinking greedily from it.

And only when she felt as if he had sucked her dry did he draw down the zip of her dress, letting it fall into a pool of rich, dark velvet onto the ground.

He sucked in a low breath of appreciation as she stood before him wearing nothing but flimsy underwear of soft green lace, her golden-white skin gleaming like silk. Her breasts spilled over the low-cut bra and the matching knickers made her legs seem to go on and on forever.

He must have seen her like this before and yet it seemed as though he had never really looked at her. Never appreciated the satin fall of the blonde hair which tumbled all over her shoulders.

'Dear God,' he murmured. 'You are unbelievable. Unbelievable.'

'No, I'm real.' She began to unbutton his shirt. 'You're wearing all this, while I'm not wearing nearly enough,' she complained.

He gave a low laugh, sucking in his breath as her palms skated light, sensuous circles over his nipples. 'You're wearing too much, oh, Kiloran—' This as she unzipped his trousers and teased her fingertips over his straining hardness. He slid his hand between her thighs and her eyes widened in helpless pleasure as he began to move his fingertips against her. 'Like that?' he whispered.

'You obviously haven't lost all your memory,' she groaned. 'You know I do.'

'Maybe it's just instinct,' he husked.

Instinct made it sound too functional, she thought briefly. Her head tipped back and she moaned again with an unbearable feeling of expectation and excitement and yet it was tinged with a sensation of apprehension.

Sex had always been so wonderful between them, but she couldn't ever remember feeling quite this defenceless—as if it would be impossible to hide the way she really felt about him, deep down. What if she cried out her love for him at the height of it all?

'Come here and stop looking so worried,' he murmured as he drew her down onto the bed beside him. 'I'm the one who should be worried. What if the accident has left me being unable to make love?'

At the same time, their eyes were drawn to his naked body, where the very visible proof of how much he wanted to make love was clear to see.

'I don't think so.' She smiled, and nibbled at his ear lobe.

But it was different. He knew that. This was a test, but not just a test of his physical ability—there was something else going on and it perplexed him. He sensed Kiloran's reservations and he was damned sure that it had nothing to do with his skill as a lover. No, there was something else.

He stroked her breasts, which was infinitely easier than analysing something which seemed determined to evade him.

Kiloran sighed, wrapping her arms tightly around his back, smoothing the flesh which covered the powerful shoulders.

He moved his hands all over her body, as if reacquainting himself with familiar yet undiscovered landscapes, and she responded instantly, her heat moist and warm against his fingers.

'Take me,' she whispered, when the longing became unbearable. 'Take me.'

The unexpected and old-fashioned entreaty was like fire ripping through his veins. He moved on top of her, his hardness threatening to obliterate him if he didn't do something about it soon.

'Oh, Adam!' she cried as he pushed into her and filled her. He began to move and a kind of sob was wrenched from Kiloran's throat. 'Adam!' she whispered shudderingly.

For a moment he stilled, reluctant to stop when something was this amazing, but he sensed that this was not the way it usually was. He smoothed the hair back from her face and looked down into her eyes. 'Tell me,' he invited softly.

Never tell a man you love him, not unless he says it first, she thought. She bit the words back and shook her head. 'It feels so good.'

Now why on earth should her testimony disappoint him—make him feel strangely hollow? But then she had begun to move beneath him, her hips writhing in expert rhythm which took him up and beyond…

'Kiloran!' He choked her name out just as she began to moan and the feeling just went on and on and on until both were spent.

And afterwards they lay there, their arms wrapped tightly around each other, neither saying a word—though both for different reasons.

He lay there, watching the moon as it rose in the night sky to flood the bed with a kind of silver radiance. Could he live the rest of his life like this? he wondered. In touch with his present, but not his past. He sighed.

Kiloran turned onto her side. A sigh was a wistful, yearning thing—she had never heard him sigh before, she realised. 'Adam?'

He turned his face. Her hair was tumbling down over her breasts and in the moonlight she looked like some creature from another world. And maybe she was, for she inhabited his past more surely than he did. 'Mmm?'

'How do you feel?'

He pulled her against him, revelling in the collision of warm, soft skin and thinking that nothing could beat this. 'How do you think I feel? Pretty amazing.'

'I wasn't talking about the sex.'

Well, neither was he, but he registered her sudden defensiveness. Was she insecure, he wondered—and had he contributed to making her that way?

'You want an update on my state of recovery at this precise moment, do you, honey?' he drawled.

She shook her head. 'Not really. I mean, I presume that what we just did—'

'Make love, you mean?' he enquired helpfully.

Why was she blushing? Why did she feel about sixteen—with all those stupid, foolish dreams that sixteen-year-old girls had? Why, if she had a schoolbook right now, she would be writing his name on it and drawing a heart round it!

'Adam, you mustn't be flippant!'

'How am I being flippant?'

'You've been very ill. We've just made love and it was probably too soon.'

He captured her hand, guiding it slowly down the front of his hair-smattered chest, and beyond and heard her tiny little gasp. 'I don't think so, honey. The body recovers from trauma very quickly, it seems.'

'But what about the mind?'

He stared at the ceiling. The mind was a different matter. 'It's still blocked,' he admitted.

'Don't you care?'

'You mean, don't I *mind*?' He laughed, but opened his eyes again and saw the anxious look which had pleated her brow into a little frown. 'Kiloran, what can I do? I can't force it—it has to come when it comes, when it's ready to come.'

But they both became silent once more.

Right now he felt at peace, and something was nagging at him, telling him that it was an unusual state for him. What if he unlocked the door to his past and found it full of demons? Would he know this kind of easy peace again? And yet, a man could not live without a past, no matter how much it might haunt him.

With an effort, he forced himself to concentrate on their conversation during a supper they had not eaten.

The memory of the dirty kitchen and the note on the table came gritting back like sand being rubbed into his eyes.

'Kiloran,' he said slowly. 'I'd like to go back.'

She stilled. To London? 'Back where?'

'To the place where I grew up. I want to go back.'

CHAPTER THIRTEEN

KILORAN waited another couple of days before she took Adam to his childhood home. She told herself that was because he was still weak, that the shock might prove too much for him, and all this was true.

But she did not deny to herself that there was a self-seeking reason behind the delay. What if she took him back and memory came with it, snapping into clarity, like a blurred picture suddenly coming into clear and bright focus?

She had grown used to this new Adam and she couldn't help wondering if she would be able to tolerate the insecurity and the emotional repression which had been necessary to maintain a relationship with the old one.

The morning she chose was as perfect a spring morning as she could imagine. The sky was an egg-shell blue, unclouded and peerless and pure. Birds sang with heartbreaking fervour in the hedgerows and the banks were studded with pale lemon primroses.

Spring, thought Kiloran—a time of rebirth. But birth was painful, nobody could deny that—just as they could not deny that it changed everything. Everyone. Nothing was ever the same again.

She shot a glance at Adam. He had recovered well, the indomitable strength and vitality of the man had served him well. Outwardly, at least, he looked the same as the man she had fallen in love with.

She narrowed her eyes. Though, on closer examination, maybe that wasn't quite accurate. He *had* changed. The grey eyes were no longer so restless. The glittering, predatory eyes of the shark had gone.

But a jolt to his memory might bring them back, surely? And the coldly ambitious Adam Black might re-emerge from the chrysalis of his coma.

'Ready?' she asked.

He drifted his hand over the silken-gold of her hair and followed it with the butterfly touch of his lips on the back of her neck. 'Maybe we should go back to bed for a while?' he murmured.

Kiloran closed her eyes, tempted. If there was one thing that Adam *had* recovered quickly, it was his prowess as a lover. 'But we've only just got up!' she objected.

'The doctor said that I was to rest as much as possible.'

'I think that your idea of rest and the doctor's are not quite the same thing.' Reluctantly, she pulled her neck away. 'Shall we walk or shall we drive?'

'Walk.'

'You won't get too tired?'

'Kiloran,' he sighed. 'I'm fine. You know, this isn't going to work if you continue to nurse me all the while.'

'I was only trying to help.'

'I know you were, honey, but the time has come for you to let go. I'm in good shape physically and I can take care of myself. And the rest I can deal with myself. I have to.'

Kiloran nodded, but she turned away on the pretext of getting a soft, woollen cardigan for the sunshiney spring day had a deceptive bite to the air. *Let go.* The two words chilled her right through and she was glad to snuggle into the cardigan. Already he was cutting her out. That was *without* any nudges to his memory.

But this wasn't about her and *her* feelings—it was all about Adam and what he needed to make him whole again.

And he would not be whole without memory, she realised sadly. She could not have a relationship with a man—especially not this man—on the superficial basis of a newly relaxed persona. That was only part of Adam.

True, he was softer and sweeter, but she couldn't keep him that way just for her benefit.

He needed to know who he really was and she needed to know whether he still wanted her once he had discovered that. And she him.

'Shall we go?' she asked.

The Lacey gardens had never looked more beautiful—the lawns were freshly cut and the scent of newly mown grass brought back a lifetime of different springs. For a moment she became the child who had run across these sunlit lawns and thought how uncomplicated life had seemed then.

Or had it?

Didn't memory always play tricks? Didn't it always look perfect when you looked back, your mind cleverly editing out all the bad bits? Wasn't that nature's way of making life seem bearable? Her mother's moods and erratic behaviour had affected the atmosphere in the house, but all Kiloran could remember was a happy little girl, running through the flowers.

They crunched their way up the gravel path to the sound of birdsong and the gentle whisper of the breeze as it rustled its way through the new leaves.

'You're very quiet,' observed Adam.

'Mmm.' She glanced up. Was it her imagination, or were the grey eyes already a little more distant? Would she, too, soon be nothing more than a memory to him? 'Can you remember the way?'

It seemed that he could, his feet taking him automatically on a route he had not trodden for years. Paths of familiarity were worn deep into the mind, he realised, and some things you found you knew on an unconscious level.

They passed the bus stop and he came to a halt. 'I caught the bus there,' he said slowly. 'To London. The day I left Lacey's.'

She nodded, seeing a contemplative look cross over his face. 'Tell me.'

He dug his hands deep into the pockets of his jeans. 'It was a grey day.' As grey as the wasteland of his coma. 'I had a pocketful of money I'd earned at Lacey's.' He remembered a feeling of lightness, of no longer being encumbered by the burden of debt, but there had been a feeling of emptiness, too. Now why was that—*why was that*?

There had been a girl on the bus. She'd had some

beads round her neck which had spelt 'love' and the kind of dress which should have ideally been worn at a ball—a floaty concoction of gossamer-gold which had contrasted with her raven-dark hair. She had been going to London, too, and she had shared her bag of fruit with him on the journey.

He had stayed with her for a month, maybe two, and for a while she had filled some of the emptiness he'd felt. But then he had moved on. He'd always kept moving. Like a shark, moving, moving, moving.

'And?'

Kiloran was looking at him expectantly and her sweet, innocent expression drove a knife of remorse through him. He must not hurt her, he realised. And he could. He could hurt her very badly. He kept the memory of the girl to himself.

'I went to London and made my fortune,' he said lightly. 'Just like Dick Whittington.'

'But you didn't have a cat, I presume?'

He laughed. 'No. No cat.'

'Here's the shop,' said Kiloran.

The village shop had changed—it had gone from selling mainly fresh vegetables and produce from local farms through to an ugly incarnation as a brightly lit and plastic supermarket. And now it was back to selling local produce. Kiloran glanced at the sign in the window which read: 'Organic vegetables and free-range eggs on sale here!' What goes around comes around, she thought.

Everything seemed so heavy with significance to-day, but maybe that was as it should be. By attempting to discover his own past, Adam was inevitably making her look to her own.

She had come full circle by moving back here, but she hadn't given any thought as to whether she would stay. She had never given a thought to the future before, but now she was beginning to realise that everyone had a part to play in shaping their own destiny.

Did she really want to spend the rest of her life at Lacey's? She asked the question, knowing that, deep down in her heart, she did.

His footsteps took him past the shops and beyond where the cottages were picture-box pretty with their fresh whitewash and their roses growing around the doors. And Adam recalled the nagging ache of envy. These were the places where real families lived. There had always been lights on in these houses, and families sitting around tables together, eating a meal. Glowing Christmas trees in the window. And he had been the boy outside in the cold.

Soon the houses became closer together. Here and there a drift of garbage floated by on the spring breeze and a group of boys stopped their chatter and stared at them with too-knowing eyes. He stared directly at one, saw the wariness and suspicion in the face of someone who had never known the innocence of childhood. I was that boy once, he thought.

They turned a corner and halfway down the road Adam stopped in front of a narrow terrace.

The house had changed. The front door was newly painted in a bright yellow colour. Not his choice, but at least someone had made an effort. On the window sill was a planter filled with a few straggly daffodils which matched the door colour. The flowers were dusty and in need of some water, but they lived—they *grew*. They gave hope.

The stone that was his heart stirred. 'It was here,' he said huskily. 'Right here.'

He stared down the narrow street and through a man's experienced and analytical eyes he saw for the very first time the other side of the story. His mother's.

What must it have been like for her? he wondered. He had been quick to judge and condemn and maybe that was natural after she had betrayed him. But what of her own struggle to survive—to clothe and to feed him?

He tried to imagine Kiloran—or any other woman he knew—in the same situation. Alone and pregnant, with no skills to find work and no access to childminders. Things weren't a piece of cake for women even in these days, but back then being a single mother must have been a nightmare. Nothing but grinding poverty and condemnation from society.

Could he really blame his mother for using her only asset—capitalising on her youth and beauty to fruitlessly seek out a man who would love and provide for her?

Or judge her because the very nature of her circumstances had meant that the only men she'd come into contact with had simply not been cut out for that role.

And *he* had been a major factor in contributing to those circumstances, through no fault of his own. He had been born. A child binded and restricted you—

and all through his childhood she might not have been the best mother, but maybe she had been the best she *could* have been.

He glanced down at Kiloran, who was still staring at the house.

He saw her face and his mouth curved into a smile which held a trace of the old cynicism. 'Pretty tiny, isn't it, Kiloran?'

She felt her cheeks grow warm, but she turned her head to meet his gaze. 'Yes, it is. But big or small, it doesn't matter—it's what's inside a house that makes it a home.'

He heard something of her own wistfulness. Kiloran might have been rich, but her life hadn't been a bowl of cherries either. Her mother's behaviour had been reprehensible at times and it must have been deeply embarrassing to an impressionable young girl.

And at that moment he realised that where he had come from didn't matter; that the man he was today was what mattered. But what kind of man *was* he today? Would he like him? Would she? The questions crowded him with claustrophobia, and suddenly he knew he had to get away.

'Let's go,' he said abruptly.

'You don't want to knock?'

He turned to meet the innocent question in her eyes. 'Why would I?'

'Maybe they know where your mother—'

He shook his head. 'Kiloran—look around you. These houses are for people with transient lives, they always were and they still are.'

She rested her fingers lightly on his arm. 'Have you remembered any more?'

He shook his head, trying to clear it because the memory was there, gnawing away insistently at the corners of his mind. But something kept nudging it back.

They walked slowly back along a different path, and it was when they came to the old baker's that Adam stopped, staring in at the fake wedding cake which stood in the window, which had been there ever since he could remember.

And it was then the floodgates opened and everything came back, in a dark tide which swamped him.

'Adam?' She lifted her hand to his face and tentatively touched his cheek, seeing the sudden whitening of his face and the tension which had tightened his features. 'Adam, what is it?'

He shook his head, locked in some strange kind of limbo as past and present whirled together in a terrifyingly vivid kaleidoscope.

His mother had gone and he'd had no one—cut adrift and rudderless. As if his body were hollow and he had had to fill it with something.

She didn't know how long they stood there for, only that when Adam eventually nodded, as though something had been completed, he met her eyes and she knew without having to ask the question that his memory had returned. It was as if someone had flicked a switch.

'You remember?' she whispered.

'Oh, yes, I remember. That's the reason I went to

work at Lacey's. My mother had left debts. My reputation was worth nothing.'

'Adam—'

He shook his head. He couldn't take her sympathy or her understanding. Not right now. 'I'm fine.'

It was as though a shutter had come down, effectively keeping her out. She stared at him. 'Adam,' she whispered. 'Talk to me.'

'There's nothing to be said,' he said flatly.

She waited for a moment, her eye drawn to the dusty bride and groom who stood on top of the faded cake, seeming to mock the whole institution of marriage. 'What do you want to do now?' she asked quietly.

He gave a smile, but some of the softness had gone.

'I'd like to go back to Lacey's,' he said. 'And I want to make love to you.'

She understood that. The need to obliterate pain through the sweet oblivion of the senses. But although her body responded instantly, her heart felt wary. There was something different about him—it was as though someone had coated him with a hard, protective veneer.

All vulnerability had fled and been replaced by the passionate predator who felt a million miles away.

Not a word was spoken on the journey home. Adam seemed completely preoccupied with his thoughts and, on a rational level, Kiloran didn't blame him. If his memory had suddenly come back and he was sifting and filing information in his head, then what right had she to chatter on about inconsequential things? His face was closed and forbidding enough to stop her trying to ask him anything really important and she tried to tell herself that he would elaborate when he was ready.

But her throat was dry with dread and longing and when they arrived back at Lacey's he wordlessly took her straight upstairs, where he proceeded to take her clothes off so slowly and so teasingly that she came when he first touched her.

And couldn't miss the fleeting look of dark triumph in his eyes as he groaningly entered her while she was still pulsing.

He made love to her as if he were being judged on it—surpassing even his usual skill and finesse and Kiloran lost count of the times she shudderingly cried his name out loud. It was the most mind-blowing experience of her life, but yet it left her feeling that something was missing.

And when it was over, they lay together, coupled like sweat-sheened spoons, their frantic hearts racing.

'That was...' Kiloran swallowed. 'That was something else.' She thought of how long he had just spent making love to her. 'But, darling, you mustn't overtire—'

'No, Kiloran.' He rolled over, so that he was lying on top of her once more, and his expression was hard, almost grim. 'Your nursing duties are completed, and I mean that. I give you leave of absence.'

Fear rose in her throat. 'What's happened, Adam? Why are you looking at me that way?'

'What way is that?'

How could she possibly say that his expression was no longer soft and giving? Not when this cool, sardonic flicker of interest looked far more like the man she was used to. He was blocking her and it seemed to be deliberate.

'How much have you remembered?' she asked slowly.

'Everything.' The one, stark word spoke volumes.

She sat up in bed, her heart sinking, knowing that she could not go back to the way things had been. It was impossible. And no matter how painful it was going to be, she could not accept a relationship on Adam's terms. It was not so much as second-best—it was probably as much as he *could* offer. But it was not enough. Not for her. She would live in fear of it ending, afraid to give as much as she wanted to for fear of frightening him away.

And no relationship could survive on fear.

'Do you want to talk about it?'

'And say what? That I recall exactly why I came to Lacey's in the first place? Your grandfather's kindness to me.'

'Your kindness to him in helping him out of a fix?'

He carried on as if she hadn't spoken. 'I know that I lived in America and about my new job. I know that I'm renting a flat in Kensington—'

'And us?' she ventured.

'Us?'

She thought that he spoke it like a word he was unfamiliar with. 'Yes, us.'

He smiled, but Kiloran thought that it was a cool

smile, even though he touched the tip of her nose with his lips.

'I know that we've been having a relationship and that it's a very agreeable relationship.'

Very *agreeable*? He made it sound like a piece of classical music playing on the radio!

'I see.'

He wondered if she did, but in the sweet afterhaze of making love his mind had been busy. 'Shall we get dressed and go and find ourselves a drink?'

If it had been anyone else, she might have thought he was searching for Dutch courage, but Adam was not the kind of man who needed alcohol to spur him on to say something, no matter how unpalatable.

She sensed that the end was coming, and that, if it was, she would face it calmly and with dignity. 'I'd love a drink,' she said lightly. *He* might not need courage, but she certainly did.

They dressed in silence, bending to pick up discarded pieces of clothing and shaking out the creases. Kiloran was aware as she climbed into her knickers that he was not watching her, the way he usually did. Feasting his eyes on her with an unashamed appreciation as she covered her body with clothes.

No, he seemed preoccupied as he zipped up his trousers and she caught him giving his wrist-watch a quick glance.

'What shall we drink?' she asked, once they were downstairs. Was there still a foolish part of her that thought he might suggest champagne, as if they were celebrating together?

'A very small Scotch, please.'

She nearly asked him whether he thought he should, but thought better of it. He had already told her unequivocally that he did not want her to nurse him any more. And with her nurturing role gone, she felt oddly superfluous.

She never drank spirits, just poured herself a glass of wine and then sat down on one of the sofas, and waited.

She didn't have to wait long.

The grey eyes were narrowed as they looked at her. 'Kiloran, I have to go back,' he said.

'Back where?'

'To London.'

'You aren't going straight back to work?' she questioned, alarmed.

He shook his head. So that was the measure of his work-ethic, was it? That he would throw himself straight back into the thick of it when he had only regained his memory just a few hours earlier.

'Not straight away, no. I need to see a neurologist and get him to check me out.'

'And after that?'

'I haven't decided.'

The word *I* had nothing to do with the word *us*, did it? She wanted to say, *When will I see you?* But if he wasn't going to say, then neither was she going to ask. She wouldn't beg, or plead—and she would not ask for what was not freely given.

'When will you leave?'

He glanced at his watch once more. 'I can just about make the last train.'

'Or I could drive you in?'

He shook his head. 'Thanks, but no, thanks. It's sweet of you, Kiloran—but I've imposed on you for long enough.'

Imposed? Now he sounded like a weekend guest who had overstayed his welcome!

'You'd better hurry up and pack, then,' she said abandoning her barely touched wineglass. 'I can run you to the station at least.'

She waited while he went upstairs and packed the clothes which she had arranged to be sent from London. Just as she had arranged to have his mail delivered to his solicitor, in case there had been something urgent which Adam wouldn't have been well enough to deal with. And once he had started to make headway, there had seemed no need to disturb the rare opportunity for peace and quiet.

Yet there were so many questions she had never got around to asking because she hadn't wanted to tire him, or to add to his stress. It had never seemed the right time. She still didn't know why he had driven here when he wasn't supposed to.

She could ask him now, and if he knew then he would answer her truthfully, but suddenly she didn't want to know. What was the point?

He came downstairs, suitcase in hand.

'Ready?' she said brightly.

He thought how much he owed her. 'Kiloran,' he began.

But she pre-empted him. She couldn't bear it if he began to say stilted goodbyes—as if she were some aged old retainer who was about to retire. 'Don't say it, Adam, please—it isn't necessary.'

'I want to thank you from—'

'Don't *say* it,' she repeated angrily. 'Please! I don't need your thanks. I was pleased to do it. I would have done it for anyone.'

He nodded. Suddenly she seemed a million miles away. He could take her in his arms and kiss her better but wouldn't that only be postponing things? He couldn't live a jigsaw life, with one of the pieces missing. And that was how he felt right now. Something was missing.

'Well, if we're going to catch that train...'

Goodbyes were always difficult, she told herself. She hoped that the train would be on time and that she wouldn't be subjected to a long wait with him while she tried to bite back her tears.

But the London express screeched into the station bang on time, and, perversely, *that* didn't please her either.

'Goodbye, Adam.'

'Just come here.'

He pulled her into his arms and swiftly brought his mouth down for a kiss which went on for longer than either of them had intended. It was bittersweet and unbearably beautiful and it felt like a closure. And when he reluctantly raised his head in answer to the urgent whistle of the guard, his eyes were filled with something like regret.

'I'll ring you,' he whispered. 'Okay?'

When will you ring me? she wanted to say, but she could not place any more burdens on his shoulders. She was not going to play jealous or needy—in fact, she wasn't going to play anything. A relationship wasn't a game—and if you had to make it into one in order for it to survive, then maybe it wasn't worth keeping.

Perhaps she should make it easy for him. Tell him that there was no obligation and that she understood his need to get away. Would that show she had some pride left and ensure she would get over him more quickly? But wasn't that just thinking about *her* feelings, and not his?

She opened her mouth to say something, but nothing seemed right, and when the guard blew his whistle again she was both relieved and sad. The moment had come. He was going, only this time it was not like a normal farewell. 'Goodbye, Adam,' she whispered back.

He squeezed her tightly one more time and then climbed onto the train and waved at her through the grimy window, his grey eyes strangely sombre.

And she stood watching the train, not moving from that spot until long after it had disappeared.

CHAPTER FOURTEEN

AFTER he'd gone, Kiloran spent the evening wandering around the house like a lost soul, unable to settle to anything, and her heart nearly leapt out of her chest when the telephone began to ring.

She snatched it up. 'Hello?'

'Kiloran?'

'Oh, Adam!' She breathed a low sigh of relief, appalled to realise that she had half expected never to hear from him again. But that would have implied a lack of courage on his part, and he was certainly not lacking in courage. 'Are you okay?'

Okay? He looked around him, at the luxurious flat which was his home. It didn't feel like home. It felt like some gloriously appointed but sterile hotel suite. True, he didn't own it, but it was more than the fact that he was renting. There were no little bits and pieces which had stamped his personality on the place. And no photographs, he realised suddenly. No snapsnots of his life and all the memories which meant to make up that life. But who did he have to photograph, apart from a mother he didn't know was alive or dead? No girlfriend had ever meant enough to him for him to want to have her displayed in a silver frame, standing on a piece of furniture.

'I'm fine,' he said heavily.

'You don't sound fine.'

What did she expect? 'I'm tired, I guess.'

'There'll be no food in,' she said automatically.

'Kiloran, I'm a big boy now,' he reminded her softly.

And she wondered whether her nurturing role might have blown all hope away. For a big, strong man like Adam to have been so dependent on a woman— mightn't that threaten his masculinity? She had seen him at his weakest and most vulnerable and that might make her a thorn in his flesh, niggling away with the thought that for a while she had seen him helpless and stripped away of all defences.

'Well, I'm glad you're home safely,' she said guardedly.

'Yes.' There seemed nothing more to say and he felt an immense sense of sadness. 'I'll ring again.'

The words rushed out as she forced herself to say them. 'Don't feel you have to. Only when you're ready.'

'Yes,' he said thoughtfully. She was intelligent enough to know that a series of superficial phone calls would serve no purpose. To either of them. 'Take care, Kiloran.'

'And you.' But this time she really *did* doubt his words. She put the receiver down slowly. Oh, he probably *meant* them, but she doubted that he would ring tomorrow. Or the next day. He would ring when he was ready, and that might be when he decided to tell her that it was over.

For there could be no going back to how they had

been, and no going forward to a future he had never promised her. Which left them in some kind of emotional limbo which was not a good place to be.

But she felt some of her own strength and resolve returning. That night she slept with surprising soundness and awoke refreshed, even though her heart was aching. The responsibility of looking after him and the worry of whether or not he would recover had been more of a strain than she had realised.

She couldn't mope around the place mourning something that had never been more than a hopeless dream. She needed to move on—that was what the self-help books always told you.

And moving on wasn't easy when you had little desire to do so. When staying put in an increasingly distant illusion seemed the more preferable option. But she found an inner core of strength and determination and she slowly eased herself back into normal living. She owed it to herself to do so.

At least she had plenty with which to occupy herself—things which only she could deal with and which she had neglected while she had been caring for Adam.

The letting-out of the function rooms was flourishing, and soon they began getting bookings from further afield.

Grandfather even rang from Australia to tell her that they had read about Lacey's in a financial section of one of Sydney's newspapers.

'Before we know it, the soaps will be a sideline!' he joked.

But she had good news on that side as well. 'I don't think so, Grandfather. We've been approached by one of the big department store chains,' she told him. 'They want us to design an exclusive soap especially for them.'

'I'm impressed, Kiloran,' he said. 'You've done well.'

'And we have Adam to thank, of course.'

'Ah, yes,' her grandfather sighed. 'The boy wonder.'

She didn't tell him about Adam's accident. No point in trying to explain why she had been looking after him; he hadn't known about their relationship and there was no earthly reason to tell him—not now, when it looked increasingly certain that it was over.

She forced herself to keep busy, and not to hang around the telephone like a love-struck schoolgirl.

She even went out a couple of times, but her heart wasn't in it, though as the weeks passed it became easier to sit in a pub with people she had known since her schooldays, and tell herself she was having a good time.

Spring turned to early summer and there had still been no word from Adam. She was vacillating between calling him some very uncomplimentary names underneath her breath and telling herself that the man was recovering from a major trauma, for heaven's sake, when the telephone rang. Some sixth sense told her that it was him even while experience told her to gear herself up for the inevitable disappointment.

It was a Sunday morning, and the house was utterly

peaceful. She was drinking coffee on the terrace when she heard the ringing and she put her cup down.

It won't be him, she said to herself, just as she did every time it rang.

But this time it was.

'Kiloran?'

Her heart was pounding so loudly that it seemed to deafen her voice and for a moment she could hardly speak.

'Adam!' She put just the right amount of pleased delight to hear him in her voice. Not enough to frighten him away, or to make him think that she wouldn't be able to cope with whatever he had decided.

And besides, it wasn't just his decision. She had done a lot of thinking herself. She knew that she needed to be a lot more proactive than she had been before. If Adam was offering a relationship on the same terms as before, then she was going to have to say thanks, but no, thanks. It might temporarily break her heart, but it would have to be done.

Because she was worth more than that. A relationship where you were constantly having to hide the way you felt about someone could never be a truly honest relationship, and Adam had always been a champion of honesty—surely he would understand that?

He thought how distant she sounded. 'How are you?'

'*I'm* all right—more to the question, how are *you*?'

It struck him how inadequate language could be

sometimes. 'Better. Much better. Can I come and see you?'

As if he had to ask! But he *had* asked, and rather formally too—and maybe that meant something. 'Of course you can come and see me. When?'

'Are you busy now?'

'As in right now?' Her heart began to thunder. 'I'm eating toast and honey, as it happens—but where are you calling from?'

'My mobile. I'm at the end of your drive.'

And she was still in her dressing-gown!

'Thanks for the warning!'

'I'll see you in two minutes.'

He had lost nothing of his cool imperturbability, she noted as she thumped the receiver down and ran out to the cloakroom, where she washed her face and hands and dragged a hairbrush through her hair.

She stared into the mirror. Her naked face made her appear vulnerable, but inside she *felt* vulnerable. She pulled the dressing gown closer and knotted it tightly. It was a silken affair of jade, richly embroidered with birds of paradise, and it fell to just below her knees. Far less revealing than a summer's dress, but underneath it she was naked and that made her feel even more vulnerable.

She heard his car splitting the silence and she walked slowly towards the door, opening it just as he had lifted his hand to ring the bell, and their eyes met in a long moment.

And the last, lingering memory of the man who had lain so desperately ill disappeared once and for all, because it was impossible to connect him with the man who stood before her now.

Adam was back, recovered and virile and heart-stoppingly gorgeous. He looked the same and yet he looked different, but maybe that was because he had once been hers to touch and he now seemed untouchable. She wanted desperately to kiss him, but would have no more dared to put her arms around him and do so than she would to have shut the door in his face.

'Hello, Adam,' she said softly, amazed at how calm her voice sounded when inside her thoughts were racing.

He had expected to feel displaced when he returned here and his expectation had borne fruit. She looked like some luscious piece of exotic fruit in the embroidered gown, her hair as richly golden as the sun. Through the satin which clung to her slender body, he could see the curves of breast and hip, the indentation of her waist and the slight swell of her belly.

He thought of the times he had cushioned his head on that belly—an act sometimes more intimate than sex itself—and acknowledged that it seemed as if it had happened in another life.

'Hello, Kiloran.'

'You're looking good. I mean, you're looking well—fully recovered.'

'I feel it.' He raised a dark eyebrow. 'Aren't you going to invite me inside?'

'Of course!' She opened the door wide and as he walked into the hall she thought that the fact he had had to ask spoke volumes about the distance which had grown between them. As did the fact that he hadn't touched her—and the coolly remote look on his dark face which showed no inclination to do so. She faced him awkwardly. 'Where shall we go?'

He wondered how she would react if he suggested the bedroom, but, while that wasn't quite the last thing on his mind, that wasn't the reason he had come here today. 'Is it warm enough to sit outside?'

'I think so. Shall I make us some coffee and bring it onto the terrace?'

But he didn't want social ritual. He didn't even particularly want coffee. He shook his head. 'Not unless you really want some. I'm fine.'

'So am I.'

He had forgotten how beautiful the gardens were, how at peace it was possible to feel in such a rural idyll. But he shook himself out of his reverie to meet the question in her beautiful green eyes.

'What have you been doing?' she asked.

'I got checked out by the doctor.' He smiled. 'Totally clean bill of health.'

She looked at his strong, hard physique—the black hair ruffled very slightly by the light breeze and the grey eyes gleaming. She thought that you wouldn't have needed to be a doctor to give him the green light. 'That's good.'

'Mmm. And I've made a career change, too.' He looked at her. 'I'm acting in a consultancy capacity. And doing some teaching,' he added, waiting for her reaction.

'Teaching?' Her eyes widened. 'As in times-tables?'

He smiled. 'Not quite. I've helped set up a business school for underprivileged kids—it's being funded by some of the bigger banks. They've asked me for some help in designing the curriculum and I discover that I enjoy a little hands-on work as well.' He smiled. 'I seem to work best with the highly talented people with a slight—how shall I put this?—attitude problem! No prizes for guessing why.'

'No.' She smiled at him.

'You don't seem surprised,' he observed, thinking that she still seemed a long way away from him—as though a thick wall of glass divided them.

'That's because I'm not,' she answered quietly. 'I knew you'd have to change direction—and I'm glad that you haven't chosen just another avenue for making more money.'

'How did you know, Kiloran?'

She sighed. For an intelligent man, he could be so dense sometimes. 'You didn't need an accident to see that you were driving yourself too hard for things you neither wanted nor needed. All the signs were there, Adam—it's just that you chose not to see them.'

'Yet you never said anything.' He caught her in the soft grey light from his eyes. 'Did you?'

'Say anything? To *you*?' She gave a hollow laugh. 'If I'd tried to tell you that—tell you anything—you would have hit the roof—'

'Ah, so I *was* a tyrant, after all?'

She thought about it. 'I guess you were. A little. And anyway, even if I *had* told you, you would never have listened.'

'Ouch,' he said quietly. 'If a man needs his ego boosting, then a conversation with Kiloran Lacey is ill advised.'

'You,' she said firmly, 'definitely do not need your ego boosting!'

'No. I guess I don't.'

She shifted slightly in the chair, so that the jade silk clung like honey to her thighs, and a pulse began to tap out a hungry little beat at his temple.

'Adam?'

He tried not to dwell on the fact that he was pretty sure she was naked beneath the robe. 'What?' he questioned huskily.

She saw the darkening of his eyes and knew what was on his mind. But that wasn't important. This was. A lot hinged on his reaction to this next question. 'Did you find your mother?'

His stilled and his eyes narrowed. Had he never noticed her perception before, or had she just kept it hidden away? 'I don't remember telling you that I intended to.'

'You didn't. But I knew that you would think about it.'

He gave a wry smile. 'You know me very well, Kiloran.'

But she wasn't going to take credit for a closeness he had always denied her. 'It just seemed the next, natural step and, to be honest, being you—I wasn't sure whether or not you would take it.'

'I didn't want to,' he admitted slowly. 'And in a way, it might have been easier if I hadn't.'

'You didn't find her?'

'Yes and no.' He saw her confused look. 'It wasn't easy, but I eventually traced her to Wales. She'd joined some kind of commune there. She had another child.' He paused as he heard her suck in a breath. 'I have a half-sister, Kiloran.'

She heard something in his voice. Something like pride and possession. He had a family after all, she realised. The one thing he had never had, for all his wealth and power. 'And you've met her?'

'Clever woman,' he murmured and then he allowed a smile to break over his face. 'Yes, I've met her— and my young nephew. Actually—' and his face took on an unbelievably soft expression '—he looks the image of me at the same age. He's a terror,' he added indulgently.

She digested this. 'So you've found some roots, Adam—someone to call your own?'

He nodded. 'My sister is a single parent, living in a high-rise flat in Cardiff.' He saw her face. 'Yes, I know—history repeating itself. But I want her to have more than that—and I'm in a position to be able to do something about it.'

Of course he was. 'And your mother?' she asked slowly.

There was a pause. 'She died seven years ago.' He saw her stricken expression. 'It's okay, Kiloran. I felt sad, yes, but more than that—a kind of regret, that I hadn't had the courage or the insight to seek her out before.' Because he had shut all his emotions away— locked them behind a high wall.

And Kiloran had started to tap away at that wall, chipping away at the brickwork, making him take a look at himself in a way that no one else had ever done.

Maybe he hadn't needed a knock on the head to force him to look deep within himself. It might have taken longer, but might not Kiloran have managed it all by herself?

'Life's too short for regrets,' she observed.

'I know.' His voice was very soft. 'That's why I've had to let them go.'

Her breath caught in her throat and she was alarmed at the selfishness of her next thought.

Why was he here today? What did he want? But equally importantly—what did *she* want? And she knew that without even having to stop and think about it.

She wanted a proper loving, caring and equal relationship—and if she couldn't have it with Adam, then she didn't want him. She might never find it with someone else, but no longer was she going to accept half measures. Living a life only half lived.

'Oh, Adam, why did you come here today?'

Had he thought that this was going to be easy? But nothing worth fighting for was easy. 'Because I've missed you,' he said huskily. 'Don't you know that?'

Her face did not betray her pleasure. The old Kiloran would have leapt on that with all the appetite of a starving animal, but the new Kiloran accepted it simply as a compliment, not a passport to the future. 'That's nice.'

'Nice? *Nice?*' He got to his feet, suddenly forbidding. 'Is that all you've got to say?' he demanded.

It was somewhat reassuring to see that not all of the old Adam had been replaced by the more caring, sharing version. The glitter in his grey eyes reminded her of his mastery, and a shiver ran the length of Kiloran's spine as she felt the slow, honeyed rush of desire.

'What do you want me to say, Adam? That I'm falling over myself with gratitude?'

'A little genuine pleasure would help!'

'Why have you come back? Just to tell me what you've been doing? To show me how well you look? To pick up where we left off—'

'No.'

'No?' She couldn't quite eradicate the alarm from her voice.

He shook his head. 'I don't want to pick up where we left off. I'd like to start again.'

She stared at him.

'To start again,' he repeated. 'With you. Only properly, this time. If that's what you want.'

'Why?'

The words came out—new for him, but old as time. 'Because I love you.'

She stilled, wanting to believe yet not quite daring to.

He wanted to touch her, but somehow it seemed important that he didn't. Not yet.

'Men spend their life fighting it and running away from it. Especially men like me. But I'm sick and tired of running. Somehow when I met you, the race no longer seemed important. I love you, Kiloran. You're beautiful and clever and kind and caring. You make me feel strong and yet powerless in equal measures. I'm in your thrall—I can't stop thinking about you and that much hasn't changed since the moment I first met you.'

A slow smile softened her lips. 'Oh, Adam.'

'Did I ever tell you how much I admire you for the way you've turned this place around?'

But enough was enough. She had heard his declaration, seen the evidence of it in his eyes. Now she wanted him close—as close as a man and woman could be. 'Are you going to spend the rest of the day paying me compliments?'

'If you want me to.'

'I can think of some better things I'd rather be doing.'

He raised his eyebrows in mock innocence. 'Such as?'

'Don't you think it's about time you kissed me instead?'

'Oh, honey.' He gave a low, growling laugh of anticipation. 'I've been thinking of nothing else.'

He drew her into his arms and it felt like coming home as he touched his mouth to hers, brushing his lips against hers in tantalising rhythm. It was slow and tender and Kiloran felt tears begin to prick at the back of her eyes.

'I love you, too. So just take me to bed, will you? Now,' she said shakily. 'Don't say another word. Just show me.'

EPILOGUE

KILORAN slumped onto the sofa and wiped the back of her hand across her forehead. 'If I see another cricket ball within the next five years, it will be too soon,' she said darkly.

'You've got a pretty good overarm,' Adam mused. 'For a woman!'

A cushion went flying across the sitting room and hit him in the ear. 'Ouch,' he murmured. 'You're pretty accurate as well!'

'Mess with me at your peril, Black!'

'I wouldn't dare.' He shot her an indulgent look. 'Jamie loves you, you know.'

She basked in the warm approbation in his eyes. 'Well, I love him too,' she said. 'Even if he *does* wear me out—your nephew is a very lovable child.'

'Yes,' he said thoughtfully.

Jamie and his mother had just been to spend the weekend with them at Lacey's, and they had had a perfect weekend, he reflected—this somewhat bizarre, extended family of theirs.

'Grandfather loves him, too,' remarked Kiloran. 'He loves reading him the books he used to read me when I was little.'

'Mmm.' He caught the trace of wistfulness in her voice and knew what had caused it. Her grandfather had grown noticeably frail in the last year. He suddenly looked a very old man indeed and the sands of time were running out for him. Adam put his newspaper onto the floor and frowned. Had it really been a year?

'It's been a year, you know, honey,' he observed softly.

Her mouth softened. 'I know it has. Just think, a whole year.'

A year of bliss—of living and loving together. Adam still kept a flat on in London, but these days he hardly used it and when he did—Kiloran was at his side.

The 'school' had excited a great deal of interest in the normally cynical press—it had completely smashed the stereotype for the public to discover that mercenary investment bankers really did have beating hearts beneath their hard, mercenary exteriors! These days, Adam was invited to lecture all over the world. A lot of the invitations he turned down, sending someone in his place—but some he accepted, and took Kiloran with him and they saw something of the world together.

Eddie Peterhouse had finally been run to ground in Singapore, where he had been planning an escape to some remote and beautiful island in the middle of the Indian Ocean.

'He wouldn't have survived there for a minute,' Adam had remarked drily. 'He likes his home comforts too much.'

He certainly did. He had managed to work his way

through almost all the money he had stolen from Lacey's, but Kiloran had been philosophical about it. Money was only money, after all. In the grand scheme of things it didn't matter a bit.

And they didn't miss it. The company had gone from strength to strength—which might have had something to do with the fact that Adam was now, officially, a director and a major shareholder—having bought out Aunt Jacqueline and Julia for a generous and substantial sum.

'Kiloran?'

She looked at him. 'Mmm?'

'Come over here.'

'Why?' she questioned innocently, but the darkening of his eyes told its own story.

'Come here,' he reiterated silkily.

They were equals now, in every way which counted—but he could still be the commanding lover she had first fallen head over heels in love with.

She went to him, nestling comfortably into his lap, and sighing with pleasure as she began to play with his hair.

He kissed her gently and lingeringly on the mouth. 'God, I do love you,' he sighed.

She knew he did, he never stopped telling her, and it was as though, having rejected love for all his life, then having found it, he never took it for granted. He had embraced love with the zeal of the convert!

She kissed him back. 'Want to go to bed?' she whispered.

He shook his head.

'You *don't*?'

He tapped the end of her nose with his fingertip in mock-reproachful gesture. 'Not yet, my insatiable little honey!' The fingertip strayed to her forehead, where he pushed away a stray strand of silken hair, and smiled at her tenderly.

'You never did ask me why I was on the way to see you from the airport the night of the accident, did you?'

She shook her head. 'No, I didn't.'

'Why not?'

She shrugged. 'At first I guess I thought it was just because you just wanted sex—'

'Well, there *was* that, of course,' he said gravely.

Kiloran thought how much freedom real love could give you. If he had said that to her before she had known how much he cared about her, then she would have been a blubbering mass of insecurity!

'I thought so!' She pursed her lips up like a schoolmarm and basked in the answering spark in his eyes. 'Then I didn't want to overload you with any more memories of that night. I didn't think it would do you any good.'

She always thought of him, he realised. Her heart was good and kind and true—the spoilt little rich girl a figment of his imagination—though Kiloran herself frequently denied that. 'You made me look around and grow up,' she'd told him once. And maybe he had. Maybe that was what the best relationships were all about—you helped each other to grow.

'So why did you?' she asked him.

'You don't seem as curious as I thought you'd be.'

'That's because I'm secure now and, even if it was a terrible reason, I could live with it!'

'But it wasn't a terrible reason,' he said seriously. 'I had missed you more than I expected to—and I'd been foul to you. I was running scared of what was happening to me and then suddenly, as I was driving out of the airport, I realised how empty my life was. How I could lose you.' He gave a short laugh. 'I wonder what would have happened if I hadn't had the accident—if things would have worked out as wonderfully as this?'

'We can't know that,' said Kiloran tenderly. 'The romantic side of me thinks that things could have been good—but never as good as this,' she added, and then nodded. 'Because things happen for a reason, Adam—I really believe that.'

'Will you marry me?' he asked suddenly, knowing that he wanted to commit to her while her grandfather was still alive.

The romantic in her had been longing for this, too—no matter how much she told herself that things were perfect as they were.

'Oh, yes, please,' she whispered, and wrapped her arms around him as tightly as if she would never let him go, until he began to gently disentangle them. 'Not right now, my love,' he said sternly. 'I have something I want to give you.'

A ring, she thought happily as he disappeared out of the room, and wondered what kind of ring it would be. Knowing Adam's exquisite taste, it could be a sim-

ple, perfect diamond—or there again, he might have
gone for something rare and unusual. Emeralds and
seed-pearls, say.

But when Adam returned, carrying a large, brown-
paper-wrapped rectangular object, Kiloran blinked.

'Big ring!' she joked.

He gave her a lazy smile. She would get the ring
later. In bed. 'Come and open it.'

But the moment she began to rip the paper away,
she realised exactly what it was and sat back on her
heels, dazed and exhilarated to see the familiar etching, and the erotic, economical lines of the bathing
woman.

She stared up at him, tears pricking the backs of her
eyes. 'Why, Adam?' she asked tremulously. 'Why did
you buy it back?'

'I never let it be sold,' he admitted. 'I bought it for
myself, or so I thought. It took me a long time to
realise that I'd really bought it for you, Kiloran.' He
held his hand out to her and she took it. 'Come on,
honey,' he said softly. 'Let's go and tell your grandfather the good news.'

The world's bestselling romance series.

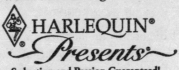

HARLEQUIN®
Presents

Seduction and Passion Guaranteed!

Back by popular demand...

EXPECTING

She's sexy, successful and PREGNANT!

Relax and enjoy our fabulous series about couples whose passion results in pregnancies...sometimes unexpected! Of course, the birth of a baby is always a joyful event, and we can guarantee that our characters will become besotted moms and dads—but what happened in those nine months before?

Share the surprises, emotions, drama and suspense as our parents-to-be come to terms with the prospect of bringing a new life into the world. All will discover that the business of making babies brings with it the most special love of all....

Our next arrival will be
PREGNANCY OF CONVENIENCE
by Sandra Field
On sale June, #2329

Pick up a Harlequin Presents® novel and you will enter a world of spine-tingling passion and provocative, tantalizing romance!

Available wherever Harlequin books are sold.

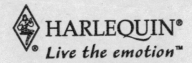

HARLEQUIN®
Live the emotion™

Visit us at www.eHarlequin.com

HPEXPJA

The world's bestselling romance series.

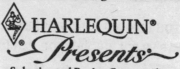

HARLEQUIN® *Presents*

Seduction and Passion Guaranteed!

Coming soon from the internationally bestselling author
Penny Jordan

Arabian Nights

An enthralling new duet set in the desert kingdom of Zuran.

THE SHEIKH'S VIRGIN BRIDE
Petra is in Zuran to meet her grandfather—only to discover he's arranged for her to marry the rich, eligible Sheikh Rashid! Petra plans to ruin her own reputation so that he won't marry her—and asks Blaize, a gorgeous man at her hotel, to pose as her lover. Then she makes a chilling discovery: Blaize is none other than Sheikh Rashid himself!
On sale June, #2325

ONE NIGHT WITH THE SHEIKH
The attraction between Sheikh Xavier Al Agir and Mariella Sutton is instant and all-consuming. But as far as Mariella is concerned, this man is off-limits. Then a storm leaves her stranded at the sheikh's desert home and passion takes over. It's a night she will never forget....
On sale July, #2332

Pick up a Harlequin Presents® novel and you will enter a world of spine-tingling passion and provocative, tantalizing romance!

Available wherever Harlequin books are sold.

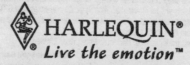

HARLEQUIN®
Live the emotion™

Visit us at www.eHarlequin.com

HPAN2

If you enjoyed what you just read,
then we've got an offer you can't resist!

Take 2 bestselling love stories FREE!

Plus get a FREE surprise gift!

Clip this page and mail it to Harlequin Reader Service®

IN U.S.A.
3010 Walden Ave.
P.O. Box 1867
Buffalo, N.Y. 14240-1867

IN CANADA
P.O. Box 609
Fort Erie, Ontario
L2A 5X3

YES! Please send me 2 free Harlequin Presents® novels and my free surprise gift. After receiving them, if I don't wish to receive anymore, I can return the shipping statement marked cancel. If I don't cancel, I will receive 6 brand-new novels every month, before they're available in stores! In the U.S.A., bill me at the bargain price of $3.57 plus 25¢ shipping & handling per book and applicable sales tax, if any*. In Canada, bill me at the bargain price of $4.24 plus 25¢ shipping & handling per book and applicable taxes**. That's the complete price and a savings of at least 10% off the cover prices—what a great deal! I understand that accepting the 2 free books and gift places me under no obligation ever to buy any books. I can always return a shipment and cancel at any time. Even if I never buy another book from Harlequin, the 2 free books and gift are mine to keep forever.

106 HDN DNTZ
306 HDN DNT2

Name	(PLEASE PRINT)	
Address	Apt.#	
City	State/Prov.	Zip/Postal Code

* Terms and prices subject to change without notice. Sales tax applicable in N.Y.

** Canadian residents will be charged applicable provincial taxes and GST.
   All orders subject to approval. Offer limited to one per household and not valid to
   current Harlequin Presents® subscribers.

® are registered trademarks of Harlequin Enterprises Limited.

PRES02   ©2001 Harlequin Enterprises Limited

The world's bestselling romance series.

HARLEQUIN®
Presents

Seduction and Passion Guaranteed!

Mama Mia!

Harlequin Presents

They're tall, dark...and ready to marry!

Pick up the latest story in this great
new miniseries...*pronto!*

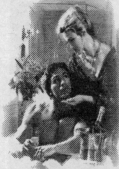

On Sale in May
THE FORCED MARRIAGE
by Sara Craven
#2320

Coming in June
MARRIAGE IN PERIL
by Miranda Lee
#2326

**Pick up a Harlequin Presents® novel and you will
enter a world of spine-tingling passion and
provocative, tantalizing romance!**

Available wherever Harlequin books are sold.

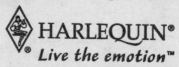

HARLEQUIN®
Live the emotion™

Visit us at www.eHarlequin.com   HPITHMA

The spirit and joy of #1 Harlequin Romance®
author Betty Neels lives on in four special novels...

THE BEST *of*

BETTY NEELS

**These hard-to-find
earlier titles
are true
collector's editions!**

**ROSES HAVE
THORNS**

**A VALENTINE
FOR DAISY**

**A LITTLE
MOONLIGHT**

**THE AWAKENED
HEART**

*Don't miss these
stories, available
in May 2003
wherever books are sold.*

HARLEQUIN®
Makes any time special®

Visit us at www.eHarlequin.com   RCBN9

eHARLEQUIN.com

For great romance books at great prices,
shop www.eHarlequin.com today!

GREAT BOOKS:
- **Extensive selection** of today's hottest
  books, including **current** releases,
  backlist titles and new **upcoming** books.
- **Favorite authors:** Nora Roberts,
  Debbie Macomber and more!

GREAT DEALS:
- **Save every day:** enjoy great savings
  and special online promotions.
- *Exclusive* **online offers:** FREE books,
  bargain outlet savings, special deals.

EASY SHOPPING:
- Easy, secure, **24-hour shopping** from the
  comfort of your own home.
- **Excerpts, reader recommendations**
  and our **Romance Legend** will help
  you choose!
- **Convenient shipping and
  payment methods.**

Shop online
at www.eHarlequin.com today!

INTBB2

The world's bestselling romance series.

HARLEQUIN® *Presents*

Seduction and Passion Guaranteed!

GREEK TYCOONS

They're the men who have everything—except a bride...

Wealth, power, charm—what else could a heart-stoppingly handsome tycoon need? In the GREEK TYCOONS miniseries you are introduced to some gorgeous Greek multimillionaires who are in need of wives.

Please welcome an exciting new author to Harlequin Presents

Julia James
with her fantastic novel...

THE GREEK TYCOON'S MISTRESS
Harlequin Presents #2328
Available in June

When Lea and Theo are forced together on his private island, he decides to do whatever it takes to make her lose control....
This tycoon has met his match, and he's decided he *has* to have her...*whatever* that takes!

Pick up a Harlequin Presents® novel and you will enter a world of spine-tingling passion and provocative, tantalizing romance!

Available wherever Harlequin books are sold.

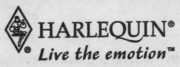

HARLEQUIN®
Live the emotion™

Visit us at www.eHarlequin.com

HPGT1